# Seasons
# Such As These

# Seasons
# Such As These.

Two Novels
by
## Natalie L. M. Petesch

Illustrations by Barbara Mueller

A *New Letters* Edition

THE SWALLOW PRESS INC.
CHICAGO

Copyright © 1978 Natalie L. M. Petesch
All Rights Reserved
Printed in the United States of America


Published by
The Swallow Press Incorporated
811 West Junior Terrace
Chicago, Illinois 60613


First edition
First printing


LIBRARY OF CONGRESS CATALOG NUMBER:
78-67506

ISBN 0-8040-0803-5


Publication of this edition is supported in part by a grant
from the National Endowment for the Arts,
a federal agency.

# CONTENTS

Poor naked wretches, wheresoe'er you are,
That bide the pelting of this pitiless storm,
How shall your houseless heads and unfed sides,
Your loop'd and window'd raggedness, defend you
From seasons such as these? O, I have ta'en
Too little care of this! Take physic, pomp;
Expose thyself to feel what wretches feel,
That thou mayst shake the superflux to them,
And show the heavens more just.

*King Lear*, III, iv

# The
# Leprosarium

he important thing to remember when first con-
fronted by the solid wall of the Leprosarium is that
it was built, not to prevent our **D & D** (Deviation
and Dismemberment Policies) clients from being
seen, but from seeing others. This is done entirely
for their own sakes, as Vita Insurance is convinced
that the best method of rehabilitation is to make it impossible for
them to see, even from a distance, those persons whose stability
and normality they once held in such open contempt. In short,
we create a nostalgia in our clients for the very homogeneity
they would once have dismissed as dullness.

As many persons have noted, the Leprosarium resembles a fortress: its rampart rises a hundred feet, its parapet is attended day and night by guards. The width of the parapet is four feet, more than sufficient for two to walk abreast. Unlike a fortress, however, it has neither belfrey tower nor crenellations, since the Leprosarium is, of course, never in a state of siege and has no need for logistical refinements: so far as we know, no client has ever left the Leprosarium without being expressly discharged by the Vita Company.

One of the interesting features of the Leprosarium is that it has no windows. This is because Vita's persevering idea in rehabilitation is that the client should look inward, not outward. Thus, in direct contrast to the Bathhouse where no mirrors are allowed to remind the client of his physical condition, in the Leprosarium all public-access rooms (lounge, dining hall, lavatories, etc.) are lined from baseboard to ceiling with mirrors: the client is accompanied everywhere by his physical self. Thus the absurd vulnerability of his body, the consciousness of himself as a creature made up of strictly decomposible matter, are unremittingly impressed upon him. We have found that nothing is so helpful in restoring a man's moral perspective as to recognize himself to be a mere cloud of atoms. Humility towards the body breeds a corresponding humility of ideas: it is Vita Company's adaptation of the monk's custom of sleeping in a coffin.

Let me put it another way: we at Vita Insurance encourage the Deviant to conceive of his identity as a construction of blocks; then, block by block, his physical uniqueness is dismantled and the client is shown the gaping hole where the "building" was; it becomes clear to him that the "building," too, was mere illusion and he is left with nothing—less than nothing: chaos. The success of our rehabilitation program lies in this flight from chaos.

While the Leprosarium has no windows (nor, I should add, any bars—we dispensed with the necessity for them years ago), there is a special lounge used by the Leprosarium Director and his staff as well as by those few visitors who visit the Leprosarium (usually just before the Annual Festival). In this lounge a limited amount of closed-circuit television is allowed to privileged "Closet" clients—that is, those dozen or so who have private cells in which they are permitted to remain by themselves for several hours a day. Perhaps I should explain that, in contrast with the Bathhouse procedure where clients are isolated except when they are permitted therapeutic fornication in the Sauna Room or diversionary play at the Swimming Pool, etc., here at the Leprosarium all clients are exposed to Maximum Gregariousness.

To fully appreciate the concept of Maximum Gregariousness, two factors must be kept in mind: (1) that the purpose of the Leprosarium is to rehabilitate Deviants who embrace a very wide spectrum of self-delusion and (2) that Maximum Gregariousness has replaced a completely ineffectual system of solitary confinement where the client, far from reconsidering the error of his ways, would have his ego fed invisibly by a continuous interior monologue and would often settle into a fierce and obstinate silence from which it was impossible to flush him out. It was often necessary, finally, to deport him to the Islands, where although it is argued that the free use of *orgone* does indeed vitiate the client's ego-obsessions, I personally feel that the unrestricted use of *orgone* results in unnecessary economic loss to the community. For instance, it is well-known that clients receiving *orgone* will remain "transcendent" for at least forty-eight hours; in some clients the *orgone* experience may be sustained for a week at a time. But the near-total amnesia and/or the superannuation of the client which usually follow are troublesome side effects. Also it is a well-known fact that the mortality rate on the Islands is already quite high (the rate deriving from what is known as the "annual lemming-effect"). The Island deportees are neither economically nor physically capable of burying their own dead: adding *orgone* to an already unpredictable situation in which operating expenses already exceed those of the Bathhouse & Leprosarium combined, seems to me extraordinarily shortsighted on the part of Vita Fealty. In my opinion, the entire Island's program needs reevaluation.

Maximum Gregariousness, however, is a viable alternative.

In Maxi-greg most clients sooner or later understand their intellectual insignificance: the thousands of persons with whom they share the same Arena (frequently there is standing room only) will in most cases grind their identities down like sand.

Indeed the great impact on visitors to the Leprosarium derives from the spectacle of these clients in the Arena. For it is one of the ironies of the program that, while the result of Maximum Gregariousness would seem logically to be maximum verbal exchange, the effect on our clients seems to be silence. Their nudity no longer embarrasses them, they stand like caryatids: silence radiates from them in nimbuses of fire. (In contrast to the Bathhouse where clients must remain clothed at all times, here, for obvious reasons, they are maintained in total nudity.) They communicate with their eyes—with such intensity that there have been times, I confess, when I feared to walk among them. It is nearly impossible to get them into a conversation, because they have learned that my assistant records all that they say. And of course such information is useful during Release Inquiries, held every two years.

For the most part, anyway, they have become indifferent to release, and some persons (Mr. Cormoran among them) have gone so far as to declare this to be evidence of the satisfaction they receive from expiation. But my own feeling is that they are for the most part feigning indifference: that they are in collusion with their beneficiaries to receive permanent compensation for their D & D policies. It is a fact that some clients, after ten or fifteen years, have been returned to their families where they enjoyed (doubtless by a system of rewards prearranged among themselves) board, room, nursing care and public parks for the rest of their lives. Yet the number who succeed at this ploy is so small that many persons, the news media among others, are always surprised that Leprosarium clients should attempt to defraud Vita Company in this manner: these persons simply do not understand how the mind of a D & D client works.

As for the silence so observable in them, only when they are in the dining room do they break their self-imposed vows. Then, in whispers, they speak to persons dining on either side of them—but never, I have noticed, to those opposite them (the table is four feet wide and extends the full length of the dining hall). Doubtless this is still another effort to keep their conversations secret; but if so, it is another indication of their failure to recognize realities, since all conversations in the dining hall are reported to the Supervisor. Without this reportorial system, the Leprosarium could, of course, hardly function: we must know at all times what plans, illusions, dreams, games, plots and "self-help" programs these clients are contemplating.

Even their childish nightmares are reported daily to the Supervisor. The flow and reliability of the reports as well is guaranteed by our "Sweets Program." Under this program, all testimonials are rewarded by an increase in rations: failure to report any suspected deviancy results in a reduction of rations. In spite of the obvious risks involved, Leprosarium clients will occasionally impart secrets to those whom they "trust," (a "trust," I may add, which has invariably proven ill-founded, since there is no reason anyone should make "Sacrifices" for fellow-clients in the Leprosarium: there are no rewards and the penalties are unpleasant—in two or three cases the offenders were brought to the Rundmarch).

Although a sense of community is encouraged as a basic Vita policy, the writing and passing of notes in the dining hall is prohibited. But this day, the day on which Kirk was taken into custody, was clearly an ill-fated one. We had hardly seated ourselves in the dining hall for lunch when my attendants promptly impounded a note exchanged between two lovers. The folded note, which was discovered in the woman's hair, read: *M. Must see you. This is unbearable. At 10. Corner C. S.* "M."s reply on the same slip of paper was simple and incriminating: *Argus is at C. The parapet would be better.* It was obvious to me from this note that the lovers were accustomed to meeting at the farthest reach of the Arena, at "Corner" C, but that they were now hindered from doing so by a new breed of dog we had brought down from the North. These dogs were a remarkable animal: with the endurance of Alaskan huskies and the intelligence of German Shepherds, they could detect overt acts of Deviation better than the guards. They were al-

lowed to roam freely in the Arena; they were well-trained in
the detection of clients who, locked in a lover's embrace, could
remain silent and invisible by night: their body odor, however,
carried easily to these new K-9's.

I looked at the two who had contrived to be physical lovers
while in the Leprosarium. It was a serious offense; but even more
serious than this was their plan to meet on the parapet. In
order to do this they would have to be overlooked by the guards:
there was no way they could do this without attempted bribery—
an offense so rare that we had no legal precedents for dealing
with it (it was simply generally conceded that such cases warranted immediate Rundmarch, weather permitting).

Thus I considered it a sign of excessive leniency on the
part of the attendants (and reported it as such), that they
waited until lunch was over before taking the two into custody.
These two, "M." and "S." (the man's name was Sorentin, I did
not hear the woman's name for some reason), were guilty of
the most serious infractions of Leprosarium regulations: a love
affair in the Leprosarium as well as (doubtless) attempted
bribery of an official. In my opinion it did not excuse them
that they were having an *hetero*sexual affair, though later some
persons thought that this fact should have been a mitigating
fact in their sentence. Strictly speaking, their sentence (three
days of Rundmarch) was not overly severe; but I confess I
was tempted to be moderate by the fact that Kirk's Rundmarch
was already scheduled for the same period. The telescoping of
events would permit Moira and me to leave for a week-end
vacation as we had scheduled.

The lovers were led beneath the wide central arch of the
dining hall where they would be in clear view of the others
who were to take note of the fact that these two had not succeeded in their plan. The whispered silences of the spectators
became more intense as the two lovers were led to confront
one another in what is known as the "Shaming Position." In
this position the absurdity of their pretensions to a unique
and personal physical "Love" was clearly evident, as it was
meant to be, but it now occurred to me that this method had
its disadvantages. That is, the offenders looked directly into

each others' eyes; a silent conversation immediately ensued, I could almost hear it, it had an unmistakable run and trill. But it was the speech of mutes: I could not understand what they were saying.

At this moment I had an inspiration. "You will turn around, not facing each other," I ordered.

And for the first time I noticed that they seemed impressed by the seriousness of their actions; up to that moment they had been acting like conspiratorial children, the very hairs of their head flowing in secret communication; and though they did not giggle the way children do, I had the feeling that the very curve of their cheeks was like a smile exchanged—at my expense, no doubt. I gave orders that they were to be brought to the Rundmarch. I glanced at my watch. It was then one in the afternoon. Unless it rained we might have yet eight hours of Rundmarch before dark. Clients are never allowed in the Arena after dark, as in their intense desire for privacy they tend to become absorbed in the darkness. Since the Rundmarch is about two miles in circumference, it is necessary to keep strict watch at all times: sometimes a client, finding himself momentarily isolated at the outermost perimeter of the Arena will fall into what can only be described as a trance of privacy. We then wait a few moments for his return to the starting point, after which an assistant is sent out to set him in motion.

The concept of the Rundmarch has been criticized by some as being pointless. The critics claim that, far from "rehabilitating," it seems to create patterns of contumacy and/or desperation. It is true that a failed Rundmarcher is transported to the Islands, in which case the loss to Vita Company is irrecoverable. But I nevertheless feel the Rundmarch is a highly useful device. Indeed it was I who first conceived of the Rundmarch as a treatment for those stubborn cases who do not benefit by Maximum Gregariousness (Maxi-greg has helped hundreds, perhaps thousands, to live happily in a society which they were fortunate enough to inherit).

I received the inspiration for the Rundmarch while on a camping trip with Moira and Duane. We were seated around the camp fire which Duane had built, and I was beginning to shed some of the heavy duties laid on me during the past few months—the Laird Building tenants and Bathhouse surveillance, and the Festival—especially the responsibilities of the latter which had fallen to me, although the honors were inevitably bestowed on the Vice President. Suddenly the bright light of the fire fell upon a circle of ants who were revolving counterclockwise in an endless procession. Fascinated by these procedures, I asked Duane what sort of ants these were (I am not one of these persons who stands on ceremony with his son simply because he has indulged his child in an education superior to his own). Duane, in that surly tone which has lately become his specialty, explained that these ants had become separated from their colony, that centripetal force compelled them to continue to seek out their colony without ever ceasing their march: thus, caught between two forces, they circled till they died. . . .

"Pretty damn dumb," added Duane, kicking dust at the ants.

I pointed an admonitory finger. "Wait. We have something to learn here."

"Aw come off it, Pop. We're on vacation."

I heard Moira suck in a breath of irritation. She picked up a stick to break up the force of their circle, after which (Duane added approvingly) the ants would "get to hell out of their circle and go on their separate but surviving ways."

I commanded Moira to put down her stick: I was determined to watch this phenomenon to the end. Which I did. I made descriptive notes of this experience from which the Rundmarch was later conceived and executed—a concept for which I received the Fourth Annual Plaque, a gold-embossed picture of the first Rundmarch clients to be fully rehabilitated by this means: they were children, and I was very proud to have been the means of arresting their Deviance at an early stage.

So much for the inspiration. The actual Rundmarch differed in this single respect: that the clients were required to march backwards, without facing their companions. This is because we have found that clients who are incapable of profiting from Maximum Gregariousness are prone to conspiracy if allowed to socialize in groups of two or three. These same clients who consider themselves above the crowd, who withdraw into silence during Maximum Gregariousness, these persons, when left with one or two others, levitate into the most inspired (to all appearances) dialogues. We have recorded several of these conversations during the Rundmarch for the archives. It was rather difficult to do so, technologically, and we were obliged to construct a temporary fence along the two mile circumference. This experiment, however, was a total success as we discovered once and for all that it is the collusion of two persons united in a syndrome of "Love," "Honor," and some third ingredient of varying intensity and/or dedication that is the most redoubtable enemy of the Vita Community.

The necessity of supervising Kirk's Rundmarch meant that I would not be able to return to the Bathhouse for a late swim before returning home, but I consoled myself with the unusual circumstance that there would be three persons, not one, and that the unpredictable combination would make the tedious process more interesting. Supervising a Rundmarch is boring and exhausting; there is nothing to alleviate the sense of time being wasted on intractable persons.

So, reluctantly, I made my way to the bleachers, shielding my eyes from the intense August sun. The temperature was well above 90 and I thought ruefully that my role as Grievance Adjuster seemed to demand that I steam indoors and bake outdoors. Then I smiled to myself as I thought of how I would greet Moira with the comment: "Tonight Derwenter returns as the *whole loaf*." I remembered at just that moment to send a message to Duane at the Bathhouse instructing him to be sure to come home directly from work, as there were matters of importance I wished to discuss with him.

I tried to make myself as comfortable as possible under the circumstances. I took the highest seat in the bleachers, where some slight shade filtered down from the temporary fence which had, as I said, once been set up within the grounds of the Arena. I then instructed the attendants to begin, as we were already a quarter of an hour behind schedule.

The lovers were promptly brought out, their wrists tied loosely together while they stood back to back. I doubted the wisdom of even this minimal proximity, as clients of this type are artful beyond words at exchanging messages. The woman's hair had been cropped. It was something which, weighed down by the pressures of my many responsibilities that day, I had not thought of myself. But I indicated to my assistant that a note should be made of the fact, and that the excellent idea should be incorporated for future use, particularly as the hair has been found to be the secret hiding place for notes, gifts, rings, and even weapons. In one case we discovered a diamond taped to the scalp, which apparently the client had intended to use after his escape: but of course he never escaped. The diamond was appropriated and three shares of Vita stock were mailed to the client's beneficiaries in lieu thereof (Vita Company has never been guilty of illegal expropriation of a client's property).

It now struck me that perhaps Kirk's hair should be shorn also; such procedures done in a ritualistic manner have a momentum of their own—sometimes not at once apparent. The act—in itself a simple one—constitutes a reminder to the offender that he is powerless: this could prevent later recalcitrance on his part. In Kirk's case, I thought, it might well dissuade him from some exhibition of false pride—an exhibition useless as well as time-consuming. So I instructed them to shave Kirk's head. While the attendants were removing all unsightly patches, bristles, etc., I used the occasion to examine Kirk's body. It was somehow surprising to observe that this man with a voice like a muffled storm had a slender, even fragile body. I began to be concerned that he would perhaps not be able to cope with even so moderate a trial as a three-day Rundmarch. As it turned out, my suspicions were well-founded: Kirk refused all food and drink on the Rundmarch (Rundmarchers are permitted to consume their rations while they march). Considering the rate of dehydration on a Rundmarch, with the temperatures always 90 degrees or above, this gesture could only be regarded as part of a suicide strategy.

The two lovers, on the other hand, appeared better able to

endure the Rundmarch than Kirk. Each time they passed each other some clear message was exchanged, but since it was neither recordable nor measurable I could prove nothing: I began to regret having ordered their Rundmarch: it would be a waste of discipline. But I had relied on an intensification of guilt through witnessing each other's ordeal. . . . I thought it would bear home to them the fact that their sort of "Love" was an internal enemy which would destroy them both; that they would be much better off if they would simply accept the terms of their rehabilitation.

At the end of three hours the lovers were still Rundmarching. But about that time I observed that a narrow trail of blood had begun to mark the white sand of the Arena. I at once sent my assistant to verify that this was not M.'s menstrual blood, as it is against our policy to allow any Leprosarium client, (voluntarily or otherwise) to disclose information regarding her reproductive cycle.

The blood turned out to be, not the woman's, but Kirk's. I at once suspected him of having deliberately cut his foot with the hope of intimidating us. Perhaps, I thought, Kirk's intention is to have the Rundmarch halted until there was an investigation; perhaps he hopes to appeal his sentence to a higher tribunal than myself.

"Didn't I tell you to keep Kirk in Total Restraint until the Rundmarch? It's clear he's managed to get hold of a sharp object. If there's someone in Maxi-greg susceptible to bribery . . . " Perhaps I should then and there have postponed the Rundmarch. But in spite of the heat, in spite of my personal preoccupations, I felt that there was work to be done.

My assistant had grown pale at my accusation and immediately hastened to see what blood was staining the beautiful white sand. I sat silently staring at this beautiful white sand rather than at the Rundmarch, hoping to calm myself with the sight. The sand is a Vita phenomenon of great interest to visitors.

It often surprises people to learn that we use the very finest sand for our Rundmarch. It seems to many Vita policyholders an unnecessary refinement and expense for persons who, after all, have so far not proven to be a profitable investment for the Community. This exquisite sand is brought by rail car from a distance of three thousand miles. The sunlight rebounds from its whiteness with the intensity of a laser. Instead of marching in a dream of shifting dunes the client is caught in a twofold fire from above and below. Without the sand the Rundmarch would be a mere military routine.

Because of this "Sunlight Factor" the Rundmarch does have this one limitation, that it must be performed in the summer. I have been criticized for the innovation of this procedure which is inoperable except during the hottest part of the year.

A brief consultation was now being held on the matter of Kirk's foot: should we bind it, or should we allow him to inflict this added burden on us all? "We are the ones," I warned my assistants to whom I give an equal vote in small matters as they have none at all in those of true importance, "we are the ones who will have to watch this spectacle of disintegration." I meant the term *disintegration* in a quite literal way, since under such conditions one hardly knows what self-mutilation the client may have in mind—but my attendants grinned and said that they could stand it if I could. I shrugged, wishing only to get on with it. It would be nearly 9:00 p.m. before I arrived home; the sun would not set until 7:52, at which time the Rundmarch (for the time) would be over: I would have put in a twelve-hour work day for Vita Company. "Continue the Rundmarch, then," I said.

At around a quarter to seven Kirk began to stagger; he was leaving a trail around the white sand; the blood dried in an instant into leaflike shapes and whorls. I permitted the Rundmarch to continue.

If Kirk was crumbling, the lovers, M. and Sorentin, were flourishing. At first I could not understand why: I was completely baffled. Then I realized that something had happened which I might have predicted, had I not been working under the most adverse circumstances that day. The lovers were united in a Cause: their Cause was Kirk. They had rallied together to help Kirk; and they were so engrossed in sending invisible and inaudible messages to him that they seemed actually to have become indifferent to their own pain. They were concentrating with a self-forgetfulness that functioned like a fakir's anesthesia.

Now this is exactly what I mean about these people. Of what consequence should it be to either of them whether Kirk survived his Rundmarch? They were a pair of purblind idiots who should have been concentrating on what could happen to them for their assistance *en flagrante* to Kirk.

I saw clearly how each time they rounded the Arena, they "spoke" to Kirk; Kirk would raise his head momentarily, like a man listening for water; then he would continue four or five paces forward without staggering, only to begin again that strange lurching dance of a man in a fever. The sun had now begun to set, but it was unlike any sunset I had ever seen; the sun, it seemed, began to boil as if the Earth were still a nebula in the process of wrenching itself free of the sun: but it would not be cool for at least a million years. . . .

But this sort of apocalyptic vision was, of course, merely the consequence of my own overheated brain. What I needed, I thought, was to go home, have a quiet dinner and forget this day's trauma. Thus, what followed is particularly painful for me to describe, as the irony of what transpired is that I was just about to call a halt to the Rundmarch. I had begun to loathe the sight of Kirk. The two lovers filled me with nausea. These were not normal signs on my part, my reactions were altogether too personal, and I knew it. So I was about to call off the Rundmarch for my own sake as well as for the well-being of the other personnel when Kirk clutched his chest, rolled in the dust for a moment, then lay motionless. I knew at once he was dead. I cursed him silently: I knew he would do it; and in my confusion I was about to rush down to the Arena myself, something I have never done as it is the obligation of the attendants to take care of these physical details of the Rundmarch. I forced myself to walk slowly down to the Arena.

I began giving instructions with regard to Kirk: the attendants were to carry the "self-mutilating client" indoors on a litter. I emphasized my words so that they would be recorded for later testimony. I sent another assistant ahead to locate a forensic pathologist to determine the cause of death, as I was convinced Kirk had died of self-inflicted wounds.

At this moment the two lovers rushed toward Kirk's fallen body; M.'s first instinct was to shield him from the sun by lying over him, holding her weight on her palms: it was grotesque.

Now I must explain in extenuation of my intense emotional reaction to this scene that, although Moira and I have been married over eighteen years, never once has she bent over me with anything resembling the tenderness, the sorrow—there is only one word for it, the passion—of this perfect stranger who now bent over Kirk, rubbing his hands and face, caressing him like a child, kissing him. Yes, the madwoman now lay nearly as prostrate as Kirk, and had sealed her mouth on his as if to blow her own life into his body. Then it was that it happened to me—that strange seizure which commenced haunting me that very day. I must describe it in detail if I can.

Doubtless it was the long bitter day of death and insults, but there in the nearly empty Arena, where the sand blazed like a summer desert and there was in fact not a tree for miles, I suddenly saw or thought I saw a leaf fall. It was an autumn leaf, turned somehow bright and sweet as fresh butter, as marmalade, as childhood—the sight of it made me want to weep. And then suddenly there fell another and another: leaves were falling everywhere, a sandstorm of leaves, frittering their soft sounds that were something between a lullaby and the luring cry of Hamlet's father—then all was darkness and my assistant was raising a thermos of water to my lips. I staggered to my feet.

"Where is Kirk?" I demanded, assuming a fully necessary and official anger.

"His heart has stopped," my assistant said. "He's been taken to the physician's office."

I still felt shaky, but inwardly calm, now that my evaluation of Kirk had been justified: a sentimental man, given to hysteria, self-pity and easy death. Like a bad actor caught in his own self-dramatization, he had died of it. So be it. It was my job to write a report, and I was glad there were a goodly number of witnesses.

"Be sure to have the physician sign a permission slip for the Rundmarch," I reminded him, and turned my attention to the lovers.

They were still standing, silent and culpable, waiting my sentence. I looked at M.'s face, drenched in tears and perspiration; at the hollows around her eyes, as though the grief she felt for Kirk had etched these sudden shadows. Somehow the sight of her face unnerved me; I feared suddenly a renewed onset of those leaves, whirring like locusts. "You understand," I managed to say, "that I have no recourse now but to transport you to the Islands." Although I spoke to both of them, it was suddenly clear to me, and I thought clear to everyone present, that I spoke only to the woman, M. *What was her name?* I suddenly wanted to know; but they had not filled out her name on the proper form . . . I now reminded them (*her*) that the Rundmarch was intended for rehabilitation, but that far from showing any modification of their habits, they had only proved their Deviationism by prostrating themselves in the sand. Suddenly M.'s nakedness was disturbing to me, and I added, although it was not really part of my duty to concern myself with such trifles: "And you will both dress at once in the clothes worn upon admission here."

Then I committed a trivial but, as it turned out, a significant error. In my anxiety to leave the Arena without looking upon the woman's nakedness again, I forgot to ask her name; and later in the day, while her clothes and other personal belongings were being readied for transportation to the Islands, I did not come across her name anywhere. Thus, all that week, and for weeks afterwards, I was to be haunted by the whispered question, followed by the whirring rush of leaves: *what was her name?* It was to become an obsession. . . .

## Love Policies & The Hall of Awards

 arrived home exhausted. It was dark by the time I pulled into our driveway. The sight of my solid brick house with its white awnings and the radiant flowers Moira had planted everywhere—begonia and salvia and asters and marigold—filled my mind with a sweet sense of release; a new herb, thyme or mint, which she had planted in a flower box, was flourishing, and it gave off an odor of upturned earth. I sat in my car for several minutes, almost too relieved to move. It was long past dinner time.

When I had locked the garage, I became aware that Duane had been sitting out on the porch all along. Observing me? I wondered. "Why didn't you speak?" I said irritably.

"You were so obviously thinking," he retorted. "Who am I to interrupt the Grievance Adjuster at his thoughts?"

I didn't like his tone at all. This irony of his reflected, I thought, a grave lack of respect, not only for myself but for Vita Community. The events of the day, I must say, had not inclined me toward patience. I was about to speak to him at once about the girl I had seen him with at the Bathhouse, reminding him of how such minor deviances could result in a catastrophe such as I had witnessed at the Leprosarium today. But at that moment Moira came out smiling. Her smile for some reason completely distracted me from my purpose: it had been many months since I had been greeted with such a smile at my homecoming.

"For God's sake," she said lightly. "We've been waiting for you over an hour. Let's not get into an argument before dinner." She placed her hand gently on Duane's head. He rose to his feet at once, as at a signal. Then Moira leaned forward to kiss me, but as she moved toward me in the darkness, she seemed to lose her balance and swayed unexpectedly so that her lips barely touched mine.

"Why don't we have a light out here?" I demanded.

"But we do have one—it's Duane who likes to sit in the dark: he says he hears the sounds better." She turned on several amber-colored porch lights designed to repell insects (I now remember Duane's having installed them last summer: had it been a year since we had all three sat out here together?) I stared at Moira: the light seemed to create a new face out of the face I knew, intensifying the gold of her hair, but softening the cheekbones. Her smile now was faintly rueful: "Let's go in. It's late—after nine, I think."

I did not appreciate this being ushered about according to a time schedule: I felt I had endured enough during the day not to be obliged to submit to any further routine at dinner time. But I was too tired to make a point of it; I bided my time. Within twenty minutes I had showered and was sitting before the fine dinner which I am pleased to say Moira never fails to prepare. The placemats were set in the symmetrical perfection I always preferred, the flowers were real, and the veal cutlets were done perfectly. I began to relax.

But no sooner was dinner over than Duane announced that he was returning to the Bathhouse: he claimed he had forgotten his report sheet, which he must turn in by morning.

He did not deceive me for an instant: I knew that he was returning to the Bathhouse for an assignation with his swimming pupil.

"There's something I want to talk to you about," I said sternly.

I motioned to Moira to fetch me some coffee; I picked up the *parfait* we were having for dessert and tried to be as casual and informal with Duane as possible; I reminded myself that he was at an extremely volatile age, when a simple act can erupt into a major confrontation. With the *parfait* in hand I strolled into the living room and invited him with a nod to sit down—not beside me, but where I could observe him: opposite me. He pretended not to understand, and stood instead—aloof and hostile—beside the cold fireplace.

"I want you to understand that your behavior at the Bath-house has been noticed, and that it behooves you to exercise more control."

"What do you mean, behavior? I do my job, that's all. And I do it well," he added.

"Too well. You are putting too much into it. . . . "

"And what do you mean by that? You—the Apostle of Duty. Impossible to work too hard for the Company. Or so I've been told."

"That's right. That's what you've been rightly told. And the first duty of Company employees is not to become involved with their clients—"

His face suffused with rage. He pressed his thumb to the mantelpiece as though he meant to leave a mark on the cold marble. Then he said: "I'm not breaking any rules. I teach them to swim. Some clients are more apt than others—" Then he raised his thumb and glanced at it in an odd way: perhaps it hurt him.

"Duane, I saw you with that girl today. Don't try to deceive me. Whatever is happening, it must be stopped. Believe me, I have your best interests at heart. Involvement with that girl means—"

"Means what?"

"—means the end of your future before it's begun. You have your whole life ahead of you. Any career in the Vita Community you want. I swear I'll do all I can to help you succeed—"

"*Succeed?* . . . " He clenched his lips on the word as if it were a horse's bit. Then he said with a strange smile, "O.K. Help me. I want to keep my job at the Bathhouse. . . . "

To me it was an admission of involvement. No young man with future prospects could want to remain in such menial employment if he were not forced to by circumstances or had become emotionally involved. I lost my attempt at calm. I ordered him to remain at home.

"And if I don't? Who will report me? You? I can see the local newspaper snapping it up: 'Derwenter Testifies.' And what will you say? That your son is in love with—"

"*Shut up!*" I ordered. I now found myself yelling. Moira had appeared in the living room. "What the hell do you know about love?" I turned toward Moira as I asked Duane the question, and her face—always pale—grew white with concern for us both. She said tremulously, "Duane, this is no time to quarrel with your father."

Duane threw himself on the sofa and stared sullenly upward at the ceiling. It was a pose I recognized from his earliest childhood: it meant that he believed himself justified, and that he would not budge one inch from his belief. I had hoped he had outgrown it.

It was late, I was due to appear at the Hall of Awards at eight the next morning. I decided to postpone any real confrontation with Duane over this matter until I was better able to deal with it. I confessed to myself that I was too tired to handle him properly. Meanwhile, Moira would talk to Duane—soothing him in her way. The best thing for me would be to go and lie down. It had been, so far, a miserable day, and I felt I would not tolerate much more obstructionism from anyone. It was, in fact, as if I were still trembling inwardly from the terrifying vision of falling leaves. . . .

I went to our bedroom and lay down on the bed. I turned to a music station which I especially enjoy during the evenings and which helps me relax. The best thing that I could do for myself, I thought, would be to fall asleep. I would write the report on Kirk tomorrow in spite of Company rules that in sudden death cases reports were to be immediately filed (in triplicate). But I was suddenly as wakeful as though I had not just put in a twelve-hour working day: my heart was pounding, my pulse was racing. But why? The work day, in spite of its frustrations, had been satisfactorily completed; Duane, though surly, had been properly informed of his duties: besides, he had only a short time left before the summer season would be over and he would return to the university. Above all, I was hopeful that tomorrow would be a much better day: an assignment to the Hall of Awards was the equivalent of Vita Company tickets to a football game: a time of pleasure and relaxation.

Yet I could not sleep. I decided to try to read myself into a stupor, and reached for a volume of *Apothegms & Poems*, really a kind of almanac, which I keep by my night table for those rare occasions when I am unable to sleep. Usually a few lines of verse, or a forthright homily will put my entire mind into a different frame. But tonight I could not locate the book. Perhaps I had absent-mindedly stuck it into a drawer; or perhaps Moira, in an excess of housewifely zeal, had placed it out of sight. I began haphazardly looking through the bureau drawers.

Suddenly my hands came upon—under the extra pillow-cases and linens which for convenience Moira sometimes kept in our room—several black lace underthings such as I had never seen Moira wear. Indeed, Moira was so indifferent to sexual matters that I could not at the moment remember when I had last seen her negligently clothed. I stared down at these articles: dainty lace brassiere, panties of translucent silk, a negligee so soft it moved under the pressure of my fingertips like flesh. The room spun. I felt a surge of nausea, my instinct was to rush out to the living room and shake Moira till she sank limp with terror at my knees. But I asserted control, I willed myself not to jump to conclusions. A deviation, yes. But not a fatal one. Guilty of secrecy, yes; of extravagance, of harboring illicit longings: but not yet guilty, not yet proven guilty, of anything else. Still, I was trembling; I knew I was trembling. I wanted to hunt further, there might be other . . . indications. But this was not the time. Accustomed to calm and quiet during the evenings, Moira would come at once (perhaps to "help me") if I began to search restlessly around our bedroom. I would wait until she was out, visiting or shopping, then I would strip the house bare to find what I needed to know. Silently I restored the clothes to their hiding place.

I now no longer listened to the sound of Duane's voice, oscillating between love and anger. His problem seemed a simple one, a solvable one, compared with Moira's. Either for her own private perversion she was wearing clothes worn only in a Vita-brothel, or she was being unfaithful to me. In either case, she was lost. This time when I lay down on the bed I could not hope to sleep: yet strangely, when morning came and I awoke, I knew I had been dreaming, but I could not remember the dream.

It was very early. Moira was not beside me. On nights when she sat up late reading or helping Duane with his home-work (frequently he and she would work out some intriguing math problem together) she would sleep in the study so as not to disturb me. This morning, at her absence suspicion washed over me like a sudden illness. I lay there physically helpless. It was barely dawn, the sunlight was threading through the bedroom drapes, and I could hear a few birds calling as though timidly inquiring whether it were light enough yet to sing. I winced at the realization that I must spend an entire day at the Hall of Awards. Ordinarily this was a pleasant as-signment, but this morning I could look forward to nothing. My tongue seemed dredged up from the earth, my head a pike. Finally I managed to wrench myself out of bed, dressed (I realized only later) in the very clothes I had worn yesterday, and stole out of the house like a thief.

On the way to pick up my Assistant, I deliberated on all the possible ways of handling my suspicions: I could report the matter to Mr. Cormoran. I could (secretly) arrange for a high-indemnity Deviation Policy; or I could take the whole affair into my own hands. The latter was risky, but would mean, at least, that I would maintain personal control over all eventualities. But for the time being I was forced to do nothing—indeed, not even think of Moira—in order to carry out the day's assignment efficiently (and beneficially) for all concerned.

I stopped at a diner for breakfast, then drove on to my Assistant's house. He did not ask me any questions about yesterday's disaster with Kirk, a professional touch which I appreciated, as it made it clear that he understood it to be my responsibility, not his, to make a full report on the Rundmarch. *His* duty was to rest assured in the belief that I would carry out mine.

Since I knew that my Assistant had never been to the Hall of Awards, I remarked that the presentations were usually events one might look forward to. On this day Entertainers and Executives, and occasionally an artist or two, were given various awards: medals, flowers, armbands. Winners of the First and Second Prize Blue Ribbons would also receive ten shares of Vita Company preferred stock. Although the stock was non-negotiable for eighteen years, it was always regarded as the highest honor Vita Insurance can bestow upon E & E clients.

"Barbara Chapman will be there today," I observed.

He was extremely cautious; he knew, doubtless, that the details of the Awards were confidential, and seemed surprised that I was willing to talk about them. At the moment, however, I felt a sharp need to talk about other people's problems. After a short pause he remarked: "I had heard that Barbara Chapman was dead. Or worse: an alcoholic."

"Not at all. For a while she had another Love-policy. But now she is back at work. Some say the greatest performances of a lifetime."

"But she must be—"

I nodded. "She is. *Quite* old . . . But that's the marvelous thing about a Love-policy."

He looked at me with unfeigned curiosity, and I allowed myself to talk more freely than I ever had. I was perfectly aware, I must add, that I was doing so to distract myself from my personal problems, so I did not at the time regard it as a symptom on my part of being out of control.

I therefore explained, somewhat in detail, that the Love-policy such as Miss Chapman had had was for Overachievers. These were clients who were several times Award Winners; but the strange problem was that while these Overachievers held up physically and mentally during their years of struggle and anonymity, for reasons Vita Insurance was unable to discover, once they had won an Award, they began to feel uncertain of their objectives and insecure about their own abilities. They began to slip . . . "Think of them this way," I added. "Think of them as acrobats whirling around hundreds of feet in the air—hanging by their teeth or fingertips to Success. They have, very naturally, a great fear of falling."

And this fear is precisely their undoing. They do in fact

begin to "fall." This is the time when they should become eligible for a Love-policy, but unfortunately the Company waits until they have "absolute proof": alcoholism, slashed-wrists, etc. In my opinion, a Love-policy should be a standard required policy for all E & E's.

But my Assistant seemed almost totally ignorant of the advantages of a Love-policy. He said that he had heard rumors that they were very hard to obtain. Except for Barbara Chapman, he had never met anyone who was eligible for one.

I assured him the policies were not so hard to obtain, but that they were never publicized. In fact, there is now a heavy fine for suggesting to any successful Overachiever that he might apply for a Love-policy. This is because the Company feels that the very idea of failure can become a self-fulfilling prophecy: suddenly the fearless trapeze artist will tremble and fall, right at the feet of his waiting and wailing audience. Thus it was, I confided, with Joyce Parker, with Clem Stewart, with Chap Anderson (who played Sir Walter Raleigh).

The one thing to bear in mind, I reminded him, is that the Love-policy is not a policy for those who have failed at love, but a Policy of Love for those who have failed. Barbara Chapman, for instance, had been an actress ever since I was a young man. She is the only Hall of Awards winner who has twice received compensation under the terms of our Love-policy (which are more than generous, I must add). She was extremely fortunate in that it was precisely during her first great crisis, over twenty years ago, that Vita Insurance innovatively offered these Love-policies to entertainers (it was only later that it was expanded to include executives). Even now there are not more than a few thousand Love-policies operative in the entire Vita Community.

Understandably the insurance premiums for Love-policies are the most costly in the Vita Fealty canon. In spite of its high cost I would like to be authorized to promote this type of insurance for our ordinary Vita citizen. After all, it's far from the purpose of Vita Company to create a hierarchy of any kind, and if a Love-policy can be of use to other persons in the Community, it is my feeling that they should have the prerogative; there are, after all, many people who are not certain whether their lives are to be regarded as failures but who may be on the brink of this knowledge: they would certainly benefit by the solid buttress of a Love-policy.

But the problem is that even though we have paid out compensation on only several hundred policies, we have found it very difficult to locate the right sort of employee to fulfill the terms of the agreement. If it were merely a matter of money, or more Vita shares, or a leisurely vacation trip, there would be no problems. But it must be remembered that the Love-policy is reserved for highly successful persons who have come to realize that they are really failures: that is, for persons who have begun to believe that their youthful standards were false, that the "Sacrifices" they made to achieve their goals were futile. Where they had expected "Idealism," they say they have found "Cynicism"; where they have expected "Integrity" they believe they have discovered "Corruption" and where they have expected "Artistic Disinterestedness" they believe they have found only "Economic Exploitation." They begin to doubt everything; their lives begin to slide off the track: a collision course ensues. The best insurance for such persons is our high-premium Love-policy.

These policies guarantee lifelong visitations from Love-guards. That is the reason for the extremely high cost of the premium, and explains in part the necessity for having limited these policies to Entertainers and Executives who can pay these high premiums. The need of attaching special employees, a secret coterie, to each "failed" policy-owner has created a virtual subculture demanding the time and energies of our most attractive young men and women. These men and women are hired on a lifetime basis, because there is no way, of course, of predicting when, if ever, an E & E client will be convinced that his success has been, after all, Real, at which time he could be expected to return to his former position with renewed enthusiasm. If this were possible, the Love-guard could be contracted for reassignments.

When a claim has been properly filed, the Love-guard then begins visitations. These visits are usually three times per week, but in some cases where the client has been very wealthy and has been paying maximum premium rates to the Company, he may have a Love-guard visitation daily. At the end of the visiting time they are required to leave. In most cases these daily visitations from the Love-guard are sufficient to restore an E & E client to his former self-evaluation, especially if the Love-guard is adept: and the Company makes every effort to screen personnel so as to hire only persons innately suited to this type of employment.

Miss Chapman's Love-guard is an example of the superior type of employee Vita Company is at pains to hire. (As I explained to my Assistant, I met Miss Chapman's Love-guard about five years ago, when the actress was undergoing her second crisis.) It had been a very long time since Miss Chapman's initial seizure, and she had paid a large sum into the Company during those intervening years: she was, therefore, certainly entitled to the very best Love-guard available. And she did, in fact, get Antonio II, the most adept Love-guard we had. He visited Miss Chapman two hours daily. During that time he was able to convince her that he adored her. In spite of her advanced age, they went on swimming parties together: Miss Chapman allowed herself to be photographed in a bathing suit for the first time in years. She began to take a renewed interest in herself: a photograph of the two lovers was "secretly" released to the press—Antonio II's hand placed in irrepressible passion upon Miss Chapman's breast, his face pressed to her throat—both (apparently) abandoned, spent, transfigured by the act of love. Nor was this consummation a mere publicity story created by photographers. The Love-guard is precisely what his name implies: he is obliged to make love, and he must be able to convince his client that it is his supreme enjoyment. Usually he has no difficulty; a client who has withdrawn into a "Failure-Syndrome" will clutch at the proferred "Love" like a spar in the sea. And, moreover, our Love-guards are extremely inventive. Those few who lack the quality of appearing "Sincere" have rich erotic imaginations and do not hesitate to compensate for a (perhaps) slight lack of intensity in their own temperament with variations of pleasure as strong as love; dildoes and aphrodisiacs, masques and orgies and occasionally, bestiality. In cases of Animal Indulgence, however, they do not employ carnivores, since these animals have a tendency to be unpredictable when sexually aroused; on the other hand, ungulates and herbivores can be trained to be at once docile and importunate.

After these demonstrations of her own inexhaustible sexuality, Miss Chapman regained some considerable worth in her own eyes. Again, she felt capable of achieving stardom. Above all, her Love-guard reported to Vita Company that she had begun to weep and babble words of tender, grateful reciprocity—a very clear sign that the notion of "Love" had sunk deep. And now today she was to receive from the Vice President himself, as the culmination of four decades of Achievement, the Vita Blue Ribbon.

As we parked in front of the Hall of Awards a sudden desire to telephone Moira seized me, a need to know where she was, what she was doing. Like a curtain rising I could suddenly see her in the very brothel-clothes she had been hoarding: standing in front of our full-length mirror, preening and admiring herself. Then as if a film clip were unreeling under my closed eyelids I saw her hand reach down into her lace panties with a look on her face such as I had never seen. My ears began ringing, as with obscene sounds. In my imagination I hurled myself at her, tore her hand away from the black lace patch at her crotch and . . . . I now realized I had been staring at my Assistant who was staring with a worried frown at me. My hands on the steering wheel were moist. When I spoke, my jaw hurt: "We'll leave the car here. Would you like a coffee? The reception bar is open."

He looked as if he did not know whether to refuse. "Come on," I chided him. "Who knows the rules better than I? . . . I want to tell you about Charlotte IV," I added challengingly.

He frowned. "The Love-guard?" The presumptuous fool was worried, I could see that. And a few minutes later, as we stood by the coffee bar, the poor fool continued to look around now and then to be sure that no one was listening.

I went on to explain that not all Love-policies were so

successfully handled as Miss Chapman's. In one case, for instance, one of our Love-guards was assigned to a client, (aged sixty), who had been an Executive in Latin America. The man had seen so many coups and assassinations and expropriations followed by illusions of calm that he had become disillusioned about the value of his work (he operated coffee and sugar plantations). He would no longer drink coffee or partake of anything sweet: he was in danger of becoming one of those religious fanatics who wears hemp shoes so as not to kill cattle. And of course he regarded his past as futile: his word was "Foul." So Charlotte IV was sent to him—a beautiful and intelligent girl who was (unfortunately, as it turned out) new at her job. According to the report which she submitted prior to her dismissal, she had tried everything that an inventive but perhaps too-zealous mind could employ: the lash, anal intercourse with variations thereof, feigned furies of attack and reprisal, the most convincing rape-enactments. But these devices did not seem to intrigue him; he sank ever deeper into self-distrust and melancholy. After a while, at first merely to amuse herself, Charlotte IV began (she reported) to have genuine orgasms. She fought against them, but there was something about the man, she said, (what this quality was, her report never specified) which succeeded in overcoming the authenticity of her performance *qua* performance. My own conviction is that she began to believe in the role of "Lover." She began to take all she did and said with an apostolic seriousness, began having immoderate and genuine orgasms: during their bouts of laughter—she later claimed—she experienced "Joy." At any rate, Charlotte IV reported that she was "In Love With" her client, and he with her. The latter was to be expected, it was part of his recovery. But Charlotte IV was instantly dismissed and removed to one of our Vita-brothels. The Executive's Love-policy was permanently cancelled; he was not a reliable risk for us. Although in this case he did eventually return to work as an Executive, Vita Company will not insure him for anything whatsoever. He is listed as a "Cannibalizer" i.e., a client who has, metaphorically speaking, "consumed" the life of his Love-guard.

My Assistant had begun to look worried. He was scanning my face with such trepidation that I realized he believed I was trying to warn him of something. It was regrettable, but I could not at that very moment explain that my information had nothing to do with him. Fortunately the celebrities and those privileged persons who had received an invitation to the ceremonies were beginning to file in. They were beautifully dressed and I felt a deep and totally unexpected shame to be wearing the wrinkled suit which I had worn yesterday. I was becoming as preoccupied as a Deviant, I thought, and wished I could forget Moira altogether. Then I at once began watching the time, wondering if there would be a break during the ceremonies for lunch so that I could telephone Moira. If not, perhaps I could find some pretext to hurry home . . . find her there . . . I began for the first time to feel I would be unable to finish out the day's assignment: I forced myself to my duties.

"We'll sit toward the rear of the auditorium," I instructed my Assistant. "In that way we will be able to report on the people who attend as well as those receiving Awards." I pointed out last year's celebrities to him.

I glanced at the Program Sheet and noticed at once that they had saved Barbara Chapman's performance for the last and that I would therefore be obliged to stay through the entire ceremony, *no matter what.*

The first nominee was Lillie Hetrick. She was a singer and entertainer of, it seemed to me then, very modest abilities. I felt it an inexcusable imposition at that moment for my time to be taken up with this sort of, as I now recall thinking of it, "Please-the-Populace" Award. Moira's deceitful eyes had turned my will to stone.

Miss Hetrick, too, had once employed the services of a Love-guard. In nearly all cases the Love-guard is young, potent, a sexual performer with the highest qualifications. In her case an exception was made: a retired Love-guard was brought back into service. His caresses were paternal, permissive—some said incestuous. Now for the past two years she had suffered no crisis and was Vita Company's best youth-promoter. She had personally recruited over ten thousand young men and women directly from the high schools for community service in the Bathhouse, in the Leprosarium, even on the Islands. Still, there were a few people who were critical of her, arguing that religious feelings lead to Religion.

For my part, I was relieved when her presentation was over. She sang the song which had brought her fame, *The Meaning of Vita is Life,* and for some reason, some quality in her voice perhaps, I thought of Kirk on his Rundmarch.

It turned out to my surprise that a young man who was receiving a Blue Ribbon Award was a Grievance Adjuster, receiving an Award for his work on the Islands. I realized with a shock that I had never seen this young man before: usually I am in touch with all the enterprising new Grievance Adjusters. According to the Master of Ceremonies who introduced him, this young man, Robert Louka, had been with us only three years and was the first Adjuster to receive an Award after so short a period of employment. A pang of dismay settled in my stomach. He was at least ten years younger than I and already receiving his first Award, whereas I who had been with the Company for years, had only recently received my first Award, along with promotion to Festival Director. The Master of Ceremonies gave his biographical data: he had just graduated from Vita University four years ago; he was unmarried (instantly, this evoked a vision of Moira and a sensation of falling gripped me). I seized the arms of the auditorium seat: he had travelled all over the world, studying rehabilitation colonies, and had innovated the present Stylobate System on the Islands. *Stylobate System?*

Here was a young man receiving one of our most coveted Awards and I did not even recognize him. Here was a young man who was being honored for initiating the Stylobate System and I did not even know what that System was. These realizations sank into my brain like an axe. I rubbed my head where the blow had struck: pain came in shreds of blinding light and then *It* happened again while I sat there in the Hall of Awards —sweating, blinded by the strange vision.

The leaves came down this time in silence, hush upon hush. They filled the air with the soundlessness of their fall; they clung and writhed together in mid-air, like so many spirits flung forever out of paradise, condemned never to alight but always to fall, into the void, falling, perpetually. . . . And I myself shrank, withered, detached myself from some barkless tree, then fell, at first lightly as a locust leaf, then spinning at an accelerating rate like some forever turning star fallen in the black hole of space.

When all the leaves had flown out of sight I raised my head . . . and Barbara Chapman stood upon the stage. She was holding a Siamese cat in one hand, a bouquet of flowers in the other. The Master of Ceremonies was begging her for a song.

I could not recall at any time having heard Miss Chapman sing, it seemed a very strange request: Miss Chapman, a great tragic actress, had a voice like a loop of pearls strung on tones harsh and strong as hemp. Yet she seemed determined to sing. She presented the Master of Ceremonies with her cat, Laertes; then, in a conversational manner, she gave us the history of Laertes' mating habits, the genealogy of the cats with whom he had been successfully mated: cats were her hobby, she said, they were more erotic than people. There was silence in the audience, then Miss Chapman sang a song, inspired she said, by having observed Laertes when he was in season. The song was entitled, *Eros, Thou Art Indeed Divine*. She then delivered several dozen lines revealing the last thoughts of a great Queen on the eve of her execution: mercifully it was over.

I do not rcall what my Assistant said on our way home together. What I do recall is that the terror on his face was like an engraving which I hung somewhere in my mind, meaning it to be interpreted later. As soon as he had disappeared from view, I gunned the engine and sped at dangerous and illegal speed to my house. My first reaction was *joy*. Moira's little Italian car was not in the garage: she was doing her shopping as I had hoped. I threw myself from the car with a strange, appetitive vigor, as if I were going, not to a disaster, but to a banquet.

Sunlight was streaming into the house, it was a beautiful

day. I somehow thought of the light as an aid, a kind of blessing
to help me root out from the dark what was hid. I chain-locked
the door from the inside, so that if Moira arrived home during
my search I would hear her trying, futilely, to use her keys.

I threw down my coat and began a systematic search. I
was determined to remain calm. I began with the linen closet,
removing every sheet, every towel, but there was nothing
hidden there. Then I made a rapid but thorough inspection of
the kitchen which had many nooks and crannies (some of
them I had built myself). I do not know why I avoided the
bedroom. I said to myself it was the one place she would not
hide anything of that sort. But I had underestimated the depth
of her betrayal: when I went to the bedroom I found, as I
had expected, the silk undergarments still lying in their hiding
place, between the pillow cases and sheets; but it struck me
suddenly that there was no reason for these sheets, we had
a perfectly good linen closet: that they were being used to
adroitly conceal what they were meant to conceal in a very
open place. The usual trick . . . . I began systematically empty-
ing every drawer.

At last, having emptied a huge box of photographs, I
found at the bottom, first in a lace handkerchief, then wrapped
in tissue, what I had dreaded: a diaphragm. In spite of my
loathing I managed to push away the paper tissue which surrounded the rubbery thing lying like a grey dead egg in its box.
I could not bear to touch it: it was a thing full of contagion
which I wanted instantly to throw into a fire, to cleanse it
of its filth by burning down to ashes.

I sat there for I don't know how many minutes, I wanted
to retch, but I only gagged silently, like an empty vault caving
in. I replaced the thing; I replaced the pictures under which
it had been buried: a blur of the past reeled before me in
cameralike distortion as I threw back into their box—pictures
of Duane, pictures of Moira, pictures of myself at the Annual
Festival. The intermingling of the past with the damnable
evidence from the present forced the loathsome question: how
*long* had she been deceiving me?

I feel I must explain somewhat to those of you who believe

that in a moment of stress I overreacted, that I leapt into a dung pit of unproven conclusions: in the Vita Community, it is the inalienable prerogative of the husband to limit or increase the number of his progeny. In order to insure against the pre-empting of any reproductive choice by the female spouse, the only permissible means of birth control between cohabiting, married couples is the condom: in this way, if the husband wishes to impregnate his wife, he has only temporarily to avoid the use of the insulating sheath. The female is rigidly excluded from all decision-making processes with regard to family increase. All details of population growth are calculated according to Income, Age, and "Seductivity;" (this is particularly true in the case of Grievance Adjusters, whose family stability is of primary importance to the community). The "Seductivity-component" is the only fluctuating figure in our "Attention-response" computations: it refers to the female spouse's attitude toward males other than her husband (on rare occasions it may also reflect the "Attention-response" of other males toward her). Females with high "Seductivity-ratings" are usually required by their husbands to bear more children than any other group in the Vita Community. According to my tabulations (made every other year since our marriage) Moira has an extremely low "Seductivity-rating." She rarely comes to the act of coitus with any natural inclination: indeed, her indifference to sexual activity of any sort is such that I have sometimes been obliged to ask her to find other means of giving me pleasure, as her indifference has had, from time to time, an adverse effect on my own sexuality—a not unpredictable result, according to Vita records. So long as this sort of negative response existed, her "Seductivity-rating" remained securely low (which was as it should have been) and did not impair our "Compatibility-rating" at all.

The sight of this flagrant instrument of birth control, therefore, was clear evidence to me that Moira was carrying on a secret affair—that someone had found her "Seductivity-component" sufficiently high to inflict this Deviation upon our family. I would now be obliged to render a humiliating report of the entire experience: there would be an astronomical

increase in Moira's "Seductivity-rating" and, a simultaneous increase in our D & D premiums.

I had never considered it necessary to have a D & D policy.
And I was fairly certain that Adultery carried on over such a
protracted period, requiring secrecies, pacts, hiding places, and
various sorts of complex arrangements, would not be considered
coverable by the usual Adultery Policy, but would be interpreted by the Board (which convened bi-monthly) as an instance of true Deviation. In short, more than a "mere" sexual
infidelity, indemnifiable by an Adultery Policy, Moira's action
was a sign of madness.

In retrospect perhaps my strategy had its weak spot: I
"reasoned," during those chilling moments of revelation as I
squatted over the obscene thing in my hand, that since the
means of their illegal copulation was hidden in our very bedroom, it must mean (I retched again as I gazed around at the
drawn drapes, the blinds louvering out the light, the soft rose
bedspread . . . ) that Moira must be receiving her lover
here. Assuming the correctness of this initial premise, I reasoned
—dispassionately, as I thought—it followed that I had to allow
them, at least once more, the opportunity to deceive me in
my own home, in my own bed . . . so that they could be
apprehended by me *en flagrante delicto*.

In a matter of minutes I had arranged everything: I tele-
phoned the Vita Company office letting them know that I
was leaving for Canada at once in order to settle a high-
premium Executive & Entertainers Policy there. And for Moira
I contrived a speedily written note, explaining that it was
necessary for me to fly to Canada at once, and that I would
telephone her upon my arrival to let her know my hotel.

Then I packed my flight bag with a few things which I
felt Moira would recognize as my usual travelling essentials—
toothpaste and brush, underclothes, pajamas, and robe. Then
I checked quickly all the bedroom drawers so that they would
appear as innocent as they had seemed before my search, and
I headed straight for the Vita-brothel, driving like a madman
all the way.

When I left the Vita Brothel, I had but one thought; to hurry home and *catch them at it.* It is my distinct recollection that I ran all the way, then about twenty feet from my house I pulled myself up short: with masterful disingenuousness, parked right in front of the house was a Company car such as is issued to all Grievance Adjusters. On the windshield sticker, however, was not my photograph but that of another, along with the usual evidence of Vita Insurance Ownership: VITA GA, and the date of employment. I at once recognized the face of the Grievance Adjuster who had won the prize at the Hall of Awards—the one whom I had never met. I now understood with a sickening thud of my guts why no one had ever introduced me to this personable-looking young man of such remarkable ability that in his first year with Vita Company he had won a coveted prize for his rehabilitation system on the Islands: a young man, fifteen years younger than I, with energy, art and duplicity sufficient to turn a normal woman into an adulteress fit only for the Leprosarium.

I do not know how long I stood staring at the tag, taking in the bitter data: 6'2" in height. Weight, 176 lbs. Blue-eyed, with a naive hank of hair curving round his brows. His name was Louka, Robert Louka. But I did not need any more details for my purpose.

I turned to the house. There were very few lights on: only a faint blue gleam slanting across the louvres of the bedroom, a gleam which I easily recognized as our bedlamp: the blue shade had been a gift to Moira (from whom? I now wondered). There was also a light on in the bathroom . . . . Moira and I were not accustomed to leaving lights on, as so many people do, to ward off burglars because, in the first place, there had never been a burglary in my neighborhood; but also, as a special perquisite the Company had provided me with an excellent Intruder System designed to prevent spontaneous intrusions by persons who might come to beg for leniency. It was this System, which could be operated from the garage, that I now cautiously made inoperable: my only problem was that I feared that Moira, who was always aware of the slightest change in her environment, might hear the garage door opening. But no sound came from the house.

I then scuttled back to the window, edging along through the grass. To my dismay Duane had done what he so seldom remembered to do: he had cleared the grounds around the house, piling up broken tree branches, leaves, and other decaying rubbish. But instead of placing it all into barrels for the next day's pick-up, he had simply raked it all together: a careless, irresponsible sort of work. I had many times instructed him to shovel the trash immediately into the barrel. I now found my feet stumbling over the rubbish. An animal suddenly leaped out from beneath the rubbish heap, and for a moment I thought it was a rat. But there could be no rats in houses built for Vita Company personnel, I should have known that. Yet the grotesque impression unnerved me: the animal—doubtless a cat—leaped like a wailing banshee across our fence. I stood trembling with revulsion, breathing through my mouth.

I crouched beneath the window sill; the leaves underfoot crackled at my weight. Real leaves they were, not a vision or nightmare, but the rustling chaos of Nature. But the sound was sufficient to arouse the echo of my imagination—as if I had only imagined the world to be real. So that suddenly the real leaves became transformed into the leaves of my nightmare: they were crackling underfoot because they were burning, because I was being burned. The flames rose, ashes rose, my body crumbled . . . . I managed somehow not to scream out against this vision. And then, as suddenly as it had come upon me, it subsided. The flames vanished. I stood again in the real leaves which were damp from the night air and were now soughing softly under my feet like whispering lovers.

I controlled the trembling of my legs long enough to raise myself up and to peer through the bedroom window. The louvres of the blinds were carefully shut, the drapes drawn to for added privacy. But I was at an advantage, I knew the house, it was my house. I knew every bend in the blinds, having arranged them dozens of times . . . for Moira and myself. He—Louka—would not know the bent louvre which frequently caught on the outer fold of the drapes as they swung to, leaving a chink in the darkness, a penny arcade of light through which one might clearly see the wretches make the beast with two backs.

And I saw it. That is the thing. I saw it all. To imagine adultery is one thing; to see it unveiled as if with deliberate provocation, with assiduous insult before one's eyes, is enough to drive men mad. Yes mad. I have no recourse but to condemn myself with that word. I am no criminal, no common murderer, but the sight of Moira, whose yielding body had lain so many nights under mine, as to the grind of snow and stone and wind, peacefully accepting, waiting, her face turned always slightly away somewhere beyond me (I had believed all along that it withdrew somewhere beyond me into a calm connubial light of her own where I had no need to enter); to see Moira, I say, transformed—suddenly aping and miming and climbing and pursuing and panting, her eyes dark with lust as those of the girl at the Vita-brothel—I am no murderer, I say, but the humiliation, the revulsion of such a sight are enough to drive men mad.

I picked up a forked branch which had been dropped or had fallen into the pile of rubbish and within moments I had broken through the window and was in the bedroom. I heard Moira scream and her scream enraged me. For it was a protective scream, a scream of love and anguish, not for me but for him, and as she threw herself upon me to break the blow, I struck her with my free hand, the one without the forked tree branch, struck her with such force as to fling her across the room. And that naked beast, Louka, was caught beneath the first blow which stunned him. I had no recourse but to strike him again and again while Moira screamed. If she had stopped screaming I might not have gone on hitting him. I might have turned to her sobbing, asking *why?* But her screams drove me mad: she loved him, that was it, she loved him and therefore she loved *it*, and with those blows I wiped from the record twenty years of her fulsome lying and pretending. Never again would she lie under my body, touch my shoulders with the patience and resignation, the passionless pleasureless coupling of the Vita-brothel. And that was the way it was. . . .

# The Islands & The Stylobate System

nd why they sent me to the Islands I do not understand. Vita Company is founded on the principle of rehabilitation, and I was offered no opportunity for rehabilitation: I was not even granted a temporary commitment to the Leprosarium, though Moira was so granted. After a Rundmarch of three days which she survived totally unrehabilitated, choking with rage and loathing for her jurors, she was also deported to the Islands. I have seen her here twice, swilling *orgone* with the rest of the Islanders.

Their argument for transporting me to the Islands was not that I had murdered my wife's lover, which they said any Vita-juror could understand, but that as Annual Festival Director, as well as Grievance Adjuster, a higher duty was demanded of me than of ordinary men: that I was expected to lead the people, not to follow them. Above all, my verdict was sealed in advance by the fact that my victim (who would ordinarily have been classified as the Deviant in an adultery suit) was also a Grievance Adjuster. Thus it became a matter of acute embarrassment to Vita Company: public opinion was shaken with regard to the authority of Grievance Adjusters generally. For a while Vita Fealty was beseiged with insurance claims, at enormous loss. It was doubtless for all these reasons I was convicted and transported: an irreversible judgement, they said.

The Company, it is interesting to note, was obliged to pay an unprecedented indemnity figure for the death of Robert Louka. The high claim was warranted by the fact that his beneficiaries were compensated as though he had been killed in an accident. But it was no accident at all. He brought his death upon himself. I was only the instrument of it. While I watched them from the window the branch fell into my hand, a forked branch such as is used to kill snakes: the tree had yielded its instrument. At most, I was a mere accessory.

So it was, as the news media pointed out, no ordinary case: two Grievance Adjusters—one of them Director of the Annual Festival. And doubtless that explains the otherwise inexplicable: that none of us was ordinary—not Moira, not Louka, nor myself—that therefore our Deviation was considered extraordinary, and the judgement warranted extraordinary punishment. Only the week before, the editorials persistently reminded us, Louka had received his prize for his reform work on the Islands.

And that, at first, was the bitterest irony of all: that this man who had wrecked my career and debauched my wife should continue, even after his death, like a haunting hand from the grave, to humiliate me with his successes.

A further irony: during my years as Grievance Adjuster I had come to the Islands only infrequently, usually accompanied by a forensic pathologist whose presence was required to confirm the numerous deaths from *orgone*. On the few occasions when I visited here, I tried to keep aloof from the spectacle of the swooning Deviants who were oblivious to all feeling but the ecstasy of *orgone*: I looked upon them with revulsion, comparing myself to Odysseus among the swine.

But after my first year—a prolonged and heavy burden of days—I began to think of myself as an Islander. I began to imitate their willing self-destruction in which *orgone* is both object and accomplice. I partook of their orgies, their long dreams, their perpetual ecstasy: it was a strange kind of paradise in which I knew myself to be simultaneously Circe's swine and the magic wand by which I could again transform myself into a man. I shambled like a boar, I squealed like a pig, I moved with the herd; yet, I continued to hover between two worlds, the world of will and the sweeter world of the resignation of will. Our orgies were silent, prolonged like secret, internecine battles; they were not shared, they were like capital gains: each one wanted all he could have, every thrill and shudder and vibration and final transcendence which would ultimately send him out of the Island in the only way he could get out, by leaving the world altogether. This went on month after month: I sniffed or drank or inhaled my *orgone* like a child bobbing for apples. I became emaciated, I could barely walk. Daily as I consumed my *orgone* I watched my skin, with a certain malicious pleasure, become a sepulchre: a true leper, I thought.

Then one day as I was shambling along a stream, watching my dull shrunken face appear from time to time on its sunlit surface, I looked up at what I thought at first was another apparition from the dreams of *orgone*. Then I was certain, in spite of my numbed senses, that the woman approaching me, walking alongside the stream as I was walking in it, was she whom I had known only as "M." At once there came a rush of memories from that Former Time, when she had been a client awaiting my judgement and it had been I alone who had the power to transport her here from the Leprosarium: again I experienced that sense of boundless loss that I had never been able to learn her name . . . . I wondered also if the lover for whom she had risked deportation to this dead dread place was also still alive on the Islands.

Apparently she did not at first recognize me; she continued to stroll along the stream as if she had no fear of my approaching figure, though I knew myself to be shambling like a shoat. Perhaps she knew that the Islanders were never violent: there had never been a report of forced sexuality; *orgone* kept us all satiated so that between *extases* an uninitiated observer might have taken us to be neuters.

At any rate "M." did not look up as she approached. I noticed how abundant her hair had become, and I experienced a strange relief in recalling that it had not been I who had ordered her head shaven, but one of my assistants. I stood motionless, waiting with the keenest anxiety her response to my presence. Would she turn and run? or would she throw stones at me as though I were a mad dog? If she were to have decided to beat me to death with a stone or a branch, I would not have defended myself. Even had I wished to resist I could not have done so. I was at that moment as weak as a sick animal: I was not even certain that what I thought was "M." was not another hallucination.

But she was real. In a moment, it seemed, I would be able to touch her. . . . Then she looked up, her eyes widened in disbelief, her lips parted in terror. Alas, what did she think I could do to her, now that I was no longer Judge, but Victim and Prisoner, like herself?

But she felt perhaps some power to hurt her was still within me. She put out her hands as if to ward me off, as if to beg me not to come further—and this above all—not to touch her. Perhaps she believed that now that we were together in the slime, I would expect her to join me in the anesthesia of *orgone*. Even Islanders who had once hated each other now coupled together. No longer identifiable as individuals, in convulsions of *extase*, they copulated as in a dream and dreamt that they copulated.

But "M." was far from being in *extase*, and my own convulsions had now run their course. I was at least fully conscious. To my surprise "M.", unlike myself, seemed in excellent health. It struck me that it must be that she had never taken *orgone* and I wondered how she had managed that on this Island of dying swine. But I could not ask, she was too frightened of me.

And suddenly I cursed that Former Time which bound my lips so that I could not speak and be forgiven: could not approach the one person on the Islands whose mind had apparently not been destroyed, who might converse with me and end my boredom. And I realized at that moment that more than sex, love, family, honor, I wanted only one thing: a human intelligence with whom I might commune. And here she was, one whom I had myself condemned and transported here. As all these realizations struck me, I began to tremble. Perhaps "M." thought I trembled with rage or madness, because it was then that she fled, her bare feet crushing the leaves as she ran. Like Daphne, she turned only once to look at me, her eyes full of terror— not turning to laurel as in the myth, but into a kind of light which glanced upon the arc of fern leaves beside her, then disappeared. In her haste her shawl caught among the ferns; the thinly-woven cloth peeled away from her as if the mere sight of me had flayed her alive.

When she had gone I staggered out of the creek and carefully separated her shawl from the fern leaves. I knew she had no need of it except to protect herself from the intense and perpetual sun on the Islands, but I told myself I would keep it for her: that she would speak to me one day and I would return it. A fragrance emanated from the shawl as of sun and sea and air: I wrapped myself into it, wound my arms through its arms of empty space. Then I threw myself on the ground and wept. When at last exhaustion had silenced my grief, I lay on my back and stared at the sky as though skimming the clouds for some sign of her. Only a fragile whiteness, like a film of light across the blue brow of sky, moved the silence. Then, almost as if I had been awaiting it, like some knell which mourns and measures the hour of grief, a locust leaf fell from the sky. I watched it skirl as it fell, it resembled the limbs of Icarus plunging into the sea. Then suddenly it seemed to try to right itself, to break its fall. Slowly it maneuvered, rising and turning like a sailboat changing its direction: then it sailed away on an invisible sea of air. I waited for a moment, not believing that this single leaf would not at once be followed by another and another till again the air would drone with a myriad insect armies sucking away my breath, covering me with their dust. But nothing more happened. A sob from my throat broke upon the silence, I began suddenly to feel worthy of following her: perhaps I would learn her name. I felt that if only she would recognize me, not as a criminal but as a human being, something would live in me, I did not know what.

As the day passed, I became more and more determined to find her. The Island was small, one could cross it in one day. Nothing remained to me but time, and even if I were to cross the Island a thousand times, I would not have begun to consume the days that were left. Though it seemed hopeless, it was neverthless an action, like some ancient rite which though powerless in itself, could if one believed in it, divert the direction of disaster. So I decided to devote myself to a patterned crossing and recrossing of the Island. The fact that there were other islands nearby and that the possibility of "M."

having remained on this very one was remote, was ignored; I wanted to believe it was possible. I began to think, to act, to plan.

My first act was to throw my supply of *orgone* into a compost heap. *Orgone* was not valuable: everyone on the Island had more than he could possibly consume. Indeed, once a year when massive shipments came from the mainland, we were instructed to finish off our allotment in a *fête d'orgone,* as it was called. The mortality rate of these fêtes was of course what stabilized the actuarial records of Vita Company by what is known as the annual "Lemming-Effect."

But such matters no longer concerned me. I only wanted to destroy every trace of my year on the Island, to start out on my search. Thus, after destroying the *orgone* (a breach of regulations), I burnt down the hut in which I'd been sleeping for the past year (another breach: use of fire for any purpose is proof of arson. But what more could they do to me?)

I did not know, nor perhaps will ever know whether what I now felt was what in Former Times was called "love." I only know that I was obsessed with the desire, with the need, with the memory of that woman. And so I started out.

In my days as Grievance Adjuster I had crossed the Island many times, but never alone, never without a detailed map of every covey of Island-dwellers, retching their superflux. The temperature of the Island, as I knew, was unpredictable: we might suddenly be swathed in a layer of humidity or glazed with burning light of the sun or bcome immersed in a fog from whose depths, as from *orgone,* one thought never to emerge. But this first day of my setting out, at least, was clear and bright. I set out with a vague yearning such as I had never experienced in this community of quick-coming death. Though it was but a nerve or impulse, it was nevertheless a kind of survival: though my yearning was a new kind of pain, it was real, not hallucinated.

Wherever a covey of Islanders was gathered, I asked about "M." describing her; but the people were frightened by my look of obsession, they were not accustomed to Energy: they stared at me in silence, as if in their drugged bliss they had also become deaf and dumb. Some stood bare headed to the elements, rain or sun; others sat cross-legged, as if in a position of meditation; but they were not meditating, they had merely found this position more tolerable than standing, requiring less effort than weaving a rush chair or building a hut. Some had simply curled up in the sun and were gnawing their fingers or sucking their thumbs. I felt such loathing for them I swore that if I found "M." I would insist on knowing from her her secret of health and survival (such is the force of habit I had forgotten for a moment that I no longer had any power, that the weight of the Vita Community no longer lay in my hand like a pestle with which I could grind the will of others to a fine powder).

One morning after I had been searching thus for about three months I saw directly ahead of me a strange flock of gulls, all sitting with their heads in a common direction: silent and austere, their grey and white plumage was of an unutterable dignity. For a moment I wished I could go with them, pull in my wings, drink in the silences, only opening my mouth to eat, only disturbing the stillness to part the wind with my wings. I cannot say how the conviction seized me, but I began suddenly to believe that these were Islanders transformed into seagulls—those few whom Circe's wand had not made swine, but who by some act of will, of resistance to evil had elected this transmigration into limited freedom. I carefully wheeled my way around them so as not to disturb their silent seaward scrutiny.

That I was near the sea I had no doubt; there was a change in the air, the grasses and trees had been bent inland by the wind. But what was strange was that instead of the coarse salt-soaked grass becoming more sparse and randomly placed, they became patterned into seaward routes, as if some surveyor had laid out the land from here to the water's edge.

And then I could no longer doubt it; the paths began to converge, their radiating lines ran into a single path. I halted abruptly. I could now distinctly hear the open sea. I dropped my bag of supplies, I stood listening with a mixture of excitement and fear. But fear of what? Could there be anything worse than what I had known? Yet my experience with Vita Company made me apprehensive; I knew that their ingenuity was infinite and that my will was weak. Yet in spite of all my previous training with Vita Company, I was quite unprepared for the sight or rather the vision upon which I shortly stumbled.

All along the frothing hood of the sea, and extending as far as my eye could see, were white monoliths resembling Doric columns which appeared to rise from the sands. At first I wondered whether these columns of stone, bleached day and night by the elements, were some prehistoric dolmens, some testimonial to Vita's past. Then the possibility struck me that these pillars were lighthouses used to warn ships away from our coastline. Perhaps every evening some Islander scaled that improbable fluted shaft and lit a flare signalling to all who saw it: abandon all hope ye who enter here.

But then at the summit, set like a tiny gemstone upon the crown of the column, I saw what seemed to be a human figure cross and recross its square entablature—a mere flicker it was, as of a shadow across a sundial: whether it was the figure of a man or a woman I could not tell, the glare of the sun as I lifted my head was blinding. Then, at the foot of this column I now discerned another figure whose pace to and fro, whose alternate shifting of a weapon, like a bolt of lightning striking first against one shoulder then another, revealed to me the unmistakable stance of a military guard. It was then I realized that this was the "Stylobate System" for which Robert Louka, my rival and victim, had won his Award. But why had the details of its construction been kept a secret? And why, I wondered, had the other Islanders never mentioned the System?

I decided that there was for me now only one course of action: to approach the guard as fearlessly as I could, hoping he would mistake the imitation of power for real power. If he recognized me, which seemed likely, as in the old days I had known most of the Island guards by sight, perhaps he would speak to me out of curiosity or even out of sympathy for my fallen condition. Perhaps he would explain to me this startling apparition: yet at the same time I trembled at what he would say, like Oedipus asking of the seer what in his heart he already knew.

And so, seeing that he had already observed my presence, I signalled my approach with an authoritative gesture. After a few tentative steps toward me, he lowered his weapon and nodded encouragingly. He had obviously recognized me. Perhaps it was the total isolation of his employment, or perhaps some vestige of respect for the high position I had held before my banishment, but I found him quite willing to talk, and in fact his manner was confiding to a degree which I would have once considered made him liable to prosecution.

The columns, he explained to me, were for those few Islanders who had been managing to avoid their consumption of *orgone*. "Now as you well know," he said, speaking with the nervous look of subordinates when addressing their superiors, "there has never been a rebellion on the Island and there never will be one." Yet, he went on to explain, it seemed that in the past year the new Grievance Adjuster (here he looked at me as abjectly as was humanly possible) had observed several Islanders who were openly expressing their rage; these same Islanders had, upon the arrival of the Grievance Adjuster to inspect their huts, shown marked symptoms of hostility and terror: it had been at once clear that their symptoms were not *orgone*-related, but quite the reverse. After that it was noticed that these reactions seemed to be increasing among the Islanders. To say that at first Vita Company had discovered ten such suspicious persons would be an exaggeration; but one day the visiting Grievance Adjuster (who had been studying the possibility of evaluating census data by a new set of criteria) reported that there were not merely ten such affected persons but more than fifty, and that they represented potential leadership for a rebellion on the Islands. Thus strong measures were at once suggested by him to the Board—measures which were guaranteed to increase the Lemming-Effect.

But the majority of the members of the Board, including the Vice President, Mr. Cormoran (and I confess that the sound of this name awakened echoes as of a clod flung into the depths of an empty well) felt that a too-sudden increase in the mortality rate would shake the community's faith in the Islands as a viable facet of Vita's rehabilitation system. It was then that Robert Louka had made his brilliant proposal. He had created for the non-*orgone* users these Stylobates on which they were maintained in total isolation, under conditions so austere that soon most had sent down messages petitioning to be restored to the Island community: those who had been so restored were now the most prolific users of *orgone*, their Lemming-Effect increased by 55 per cent, he added.

Then with a conspiratorial manner which I could never have anticipated, he handed me his binoculars. "Look up there at that one. . . . She's new," he said. "We corralled her about noon of Islander's Day. We spotted her at once because she was following the stream by herself—not a soul with her. . . . "

My hands were trembling as I took the binoculars, but I dared not look at him to see what official interpretation he might make of my excitement.

Gripping the binoculars like a buoy, I raised my head for a view of the woman on the column, and felt at that moment what can only be described as "love." I wanted instantly to be where that exiled presence was. I wanted to conceal her from the view of the guard who regarded her as an interesting sort of deviant whom they had put under his unique control, wanted above all to speak to her and explain how it had all happened. . . .

And perhaps that is really the purpose of this record, to explain how it all happened.

While I stood holding the binoculars, standing as if transfixed to the thin line of beach which held us, the guard continued to describe their System: he was treating me, I realized, as if from habits of deference I remained in his eyes the visiting Grievance Adjuster on tour. He explained to me that although the Stylobates had been instituted as an ultimate punishment a new sort of problem was now developing: what had begun as a punishment had created in a few a climate of contentment: that there were three or four persons who seemed absolutely to prefer their slab of stone, their total isolation. They seemed even to be carrying on a sort of social existence, no one knew how. . . . Vita Company did not know what to do about them—particularly since Louka . . (here the guard looked off in a non-committal way) since Louka's plans had never been fully realized and Vita did not know what further developments he may have intended.

I stood for a moment watching the frail figure whose garments were moving now in the slight easterly wind; I could see her hair, rough and unattended. I could see her face, darkened and scarred by the winds; almost, I believed I could see the concentrated look of her eyes as she gazed seaward: an intense look of communion.

I returned the binoculars—trying to conceal my triumph: there was a way, then, to reach her. And I would find it. I thanked the guard and turned away; he made no move to detain me, and I began to march back in what must have seemed to him a very plausible direction—toward the huts of the *orgone* community. Only this time I made a special effort to follow the stream until I reached the point where I had first seen "M." And there I camped . . . . and waited for them, luring them with my isolation.

They came to arrest me one day while I sat by the stream watching a school of minnows dart about in the sunlight. The ones who had been sent to arrest me had not dressed in any military garb: a less knowledgeable observer would have taken them for a group of orgonists trouping happily in the water, preparing for still another dalliance. But I had worked for Vita too long not to know their knowing ways, the slight hesitancy of their walk, like jungle cats who can well abide their time.

I pretended to doze at first so that they would have no trouble seizing me, but I realized my mistake at once: it would seem to them that if I were asleep that perhaps I had mended my ways, perhaps I had accepted *orgone* as a blessing. So I now reared up with a consciously buoyant step, I made myself ridiculously large: I stretched, marched, hummed under my breath. I even leaped into the stream, washing my body, lifting my face to the sun, my eyes (as they must appear to them) alert and awake. And then I began to sing lustily.

As I suspected, it was the spontaneous song which convinced them: no orgonist ever bursts into song: he drones, he muses, he dreams, but he neither kills nor sings. When they approached, I pretended to resist. As I had intended, in the fact of my resistance they had a rationale for attack. Their weapons came out, they leaped and struck at me, and I went down, down, into what I believe was my first real *extase* since being transported to the Islands: all my years of experience with Vita Company made me as certain as the sun shone that they could do only one thing with me now. And that punishment was my one desire.

*   *   *

Which was fulfilled. I regained consciousness with a thrill of pure pleasure as the sun hit my eyes; for the sea lay before me, a shawl of blue light, and at eye level, and to the right and left of me as far as I could see were white columns gleaming in the Attic light. Like "M." I was alone on my pillar of silence.

How long have I been here? I am not certain. It does not concern me. Neither do I concern myself with the nights, chill as the desert air, gales of wind, nor withering sun. The season here is my only change: by an act of will I have leaped into the eternal silence—from an illusory pleasure into this certain anguish. And yet, by some alembic I am content.

For one thing, now I have silently asked, and she has told me: her name. *Margaret.* You will ask how it is that, separated in space by sea and air, one hundred feet nearer the bowl of heaven, I have managed to learn what she could not, would not ever, have revealed to me while we were below among the orgonists.

And I can only tell you that mysteries occur on these stones, beneath this burning sun. At first we were only able to communicate in lines remembered from Former Days. When I received her name I asked into the speaking air: *Margaret,*

*are you grieving?* And after many hours of silence her answer filtered through my senses: *Bright shootes of everlastingness.* Which I first heard and then more and more clearly understood. That I heard is one mystery, but that I understood is an even greater. But since then there have been other miracles: we have learned to see through the darkness and hear through the rains and thus we now continuously exchange through the silent air our stories, our memories, our forgiveness, our love.

# The Long Hot Summers
# of Yasha K.

n the Detroit Riot of '43, Moseley had said that the city was burning. But that had not been true, Yasha reflected. While it had been true that all the store fronts were a rubble of glass and wood and that what could not be destroyed by rock had been burned, nevertheless, miraculously no major conflagration had begun. Even the sporadic fires which had been set in the windows had begun to gutter and hiss: it had not been their hour for *the fire next time* after all.

When finally they had reached Papa's store Moseley had pulled up with a tortured groan, as if he had come this far willingly, but now common sense was beginning to take over. They could both see at once that the Kalokovich store was a shambles.

They left the car doors open, ready to escape again at once if necessary; it was almost too dark to see anymore but fortunately Moseley had a flashlight. Yasha tried not to look as if he needed help as he staggered over the rubble and glass, but he was glad to have Moseley grab him by the arm.

A quick glance at the front of the store revealed that Papa had naively locked and barred the door. Jacob Kalokovich was nowhere to be seen. A small Philco radio lying overturned on a lard barrel loudly proclaimed news of the riot: " . . . worse since the St. Louis riot of 1917 . . . Detroit's first major riot since 1863 when during the Civil War. . . . Mayor Jeffries has asked Governor Kelly to declare martial law. . . . Hope that President Roosevelt will make a statement before midnight. . . ."

"Papa!" Yasha yelled as he ran first to the small kitchen at the rear of the store. But it was empty; only the water kept for dressing chickens was still boiling; under it the fire of the small single-burner stove flamed in the darkness.

The place seemed deserted; but in response to Yasha's cry they could just faintly make out an odd banging, as of someone knocking on a pipe in another part of the store.

Moseley touched his arm: "Somebody's back there, where the chicken coops are."

Without stopping to ask themselves if perhaps snipers had hidden in the wrecked store, they plunged their way through overturned bins of dried corn and grits and beans, to where Yasha could now hear Papa's voice yelling over and over: "I'm here! I'm here!"

Papa turned out to be screened from their view by several thicknesses of chicken wire, so that at first they could hear but could not locate his exact position. He seemed to be surrounded by cages full of grey and black Dominic hens who were fluttering and clucking with excitement.

Moseley spotted his flashlight into the corner, and in the same circle of light as Papa and his chickens they saw a black man who at first sight seemed to be on his knees, begging for his life. A moment later they realized that the man was already

dead. Papa sat as if protectively in front of the body, his wrists
on his knees, a .38 lying loose in his hand.

Papa had begun explaining at once: "He was stealing my
chickens. I knew they couldn't come from the front. The front,
I was watching. So I figured, when I heard the dog barking, I
knew right away: looters. In the back room."

Perhaps it was fortunate that at that moment a policeman
had arrived on the scene, for Yasha had wrestled with such a
combination of emotions that he had simply stood staring speech-
less at Papa, not even rejoicing to find him alive . . .

"Goddam, who shot this nigger?" the cop had demanded
at once of the three of them. He turned toward Papa, who
was struggling to his feet (neither Moseley nor Yasha had
stirred to help him, Yasha now unexpectedly recalled). "Was
he after your stuff? Was it self-defense? Did he have a gun?
a knife?" He glared fiercely at Moseley, as if he wished there
were some way he could convict him on the spot of the murder
of this black man.

In response to the policeman's questions, Papa began his
recitative, as if he had prepared it all years ago, when he had
first settled in America:

"A gun? How do I know? Did I search him? Am I a
policeman? Should I wait to see, he had a gun or no? No. I
heard the dog bark—where is she anyway? Yasha, did you see
Queenie out front? and the chickens started to fly around the
coop, very excited. I thought 'some black son of bitch,' " here
Papa paused, a vaguely distracted look came into his eyes, " 'who
knows what he'll do? There might be a gang of them,' I
thought." He turned his face deliberately away from Moseley
and stared down at the body, as if it might begin moving
again.

The policeman turned over the dead man and began strip-
ping him of identity tags. There was no money. From his shirt
he removed a small bronze pin which read: "Driving Ten Years
Without An Accident. Silvercup Bread." There was also a
Sheaffer fountain pen with the inscription: "Sonny Wilson,
Northeastern High. 14 Karat."

"They sure buy themselves the best," commented the police-

62

man, and formally passed around the papers he had removed
from the black man's wallet, as though he were issuing a death
certificate. The I.D. card informed them that Richard Wilson
was aged 39, 5'10" and weighed 160 pounds. "In the event
of accident," the I.D. requested, "notify Mrs. Ima Wilson, 2901
Russell Street." There was an outdoor snapshot of Mrs. Wilson
standing with her arms around two children. "That's all," said
the cop abruptly. "I'll take those things. Just a good idea to
show there was no money on him when I got here. . . . Now
you clear out of here, all of you, till the ambulance comes."

The three men had staggered out into the darkness of Hastings Street. Everywhere were the sounds of sirens and the rattle
of glass. Looters had begun filling their pockets with shoes
from the Florsheim store across the street. People were walking
away looking like shoe trees, with leather growths sprouting
from out of their pockets, and piles of shoes in their arms.

At the sidewalk Papa turned and surveyed the wreck of his
store. As he gazed at the smashed and depredated meat counters,
the emptied shelves, the overturned barrels of grits and beans,
at the cakes and onions, bread, cabbages and canned goods all
in an insane little pile on the floor, he covered his face. Then
he stooped and picked up a piece of broken glass, staring mourn-
fully into the faint reflection it gave off in the twilight of
Hastings Street.

"Twenty years I've been here—why did they do this to me?
I treated them like my own family. When they needed it, I gave
them credit, they shouldn't starve. I carried their debts myself,
as true as I live. Ask them. Ask the woman who lives upstairs—
right there—she's lived there all her life—did we ever have a
cross word? And now they ruin me, my business. I'm a bank-
rupt man. . . ."

"Stop it, Papa! For God's sake, can't you stop it? Who gives
a shit about your peas and potatoes?"

Papa drew himself up. Instantly his mournful voice vanished
and in its place came the proud tones of the scholar. "What
do you mean, using that kind of language to me, your father?
Is *this* what you're learning now in the college? Is this the respect the Talmud teaches? When I was a *yeshiva bocher*—"

"When you were a *yeshiva bocher,* this goddammed world was a melting pot—now it's a volcano and it's going to erupt right on top of our heads—can't you see that?" As Papa turned his head away in obstinate silence, Yasha yelled: "For Chrissake, you've just killed an innocent man! Doesn't that mean something to you?"

Papa reared his head back: "Innocent! A robber he was! A cholera on his head! What kind of a man breaks into the store to steal? Only a thief and a robber. They used to hang thieves, no? Now you want I should give him a medal, maybe, he broke into my store?"

Yasha groaned. Shouting made the blood rise, made the pain in his head beat like bongo drums. "He didn't even have a gun," he managed to say at last, his voice trembling.

Papa plunged once again into his recitative: "Did I know that? Did I know he didn't have a gun? I was protecting myself. . . . You heard the policeman. He said 'self-defense.' You'd rather your own father got killed than a miserable *schwartze?*" He shot Moseley a look of cold and jealous fury.

Somehow the word *schwartze* had always angered Yasha, perhaps because some of the most *civilized* people in the world used it, not just rednecks who had found a euphemism for nigger, but gentle people who claimed to be against war, racism and violence, survivors of Treblinka, Auschwitz and Maidanek. Yasha had put out his hand as if to stop Papa from incriminating himself any further: "Please. . . . " he said weakly, and turned toward Moseley to indicate that they had better go: and quickly:

" 'Please?' Please, what? Now you show your real self. I tell you the man came to rob me of my chickens and you say, 'Please, Papa. . . . ' You think it's some kind of etiquette game we're playing here? It's life-and-death on Hastings Street. What kind of a father is it, goes out to steal chickens? He should find another job, put bread in his children's mouth, that's what a father is. Like I did. Let him work like I worked, 18 hours a day, all my life. I never stole anybody's chickens."

"So it was for the chickens," Yasha whispered. "It was for the murderous privilege of defending your goddam property—"

"Property? A chicken is property? Was it worth two dollars'

stolen poultry for him to get killed? Only a nigger would be so stupid."

Yasha shot a fierce cracking fist into his own left hand. He looked at Papa as he might have looked at war criminals being tried for atrocities, numberless atrocities. . . .

"Don't you ever let me hear you use that word again as long as you live! Not so long as I'm around to hear it!"

"Don't yell at me!" yelled Kalokovich. "What do you mean, murderous privilege? I defended myself, my rights, didn't I? You heard him—the policeman himself said that. The law is on my side, not on the side of thieves and robbers. I don't want to hear any more about this. So long as you're in my family, so long as you eat, sleep and crap in *my* house, I treat you like a son, *act* like a son—"

"I can't . . . Papa," Yasha said slowly, as if he were giving sworn but unwilling testimony.

"Can't act like a son? You prefer *schwartzes* to your own people?"

"It's not that—"

"*Nu*? What is it, then?"

"It's a question of rights—"

Yasha was unprepared for the wrath this response had evoked: "Rights, hah! *Gehe in drerd* with your rights. I'll see every one of them dead and in hell before I'll let them rob me in my own store."

"O.K. That does it then," Yasha said solemnly and had turned toward Moseley, placing his hand on his shoulder.

Papa's face had crumpled then, and he had begun to weep and cry out in Yiddish as if in hope that the language of his people forever in exile might move Yasha to pity: "*Es ist fur wass ich habe gekommen zu America, mein sohn zu verlieren?*"

"Papa, why are you crying? It's not as if—" He had not dared continue, fearful that Papa's words were in fact prophetic —that Jacob Kalokovich had come to America only to lose his son there. . . .

"*Fur wass weinn ich? Ich sehe—du mir hasst . . .* "

"I don't hate you. But I do hate what you called *him*."

At this Papa turned a cold and jealous look of fury upon

Moseley. "Him! That black devil! *He* decides for you what's right and what's wrong? Listen to me, Yasha, and mark my words. You'll fight for your own children someday. You'll understand better what *naches* is . . . . " Perhaps Papa had sensed a tremor of response to that word which expressed all the love and pride Jews have felt for their children, because he had closed in then for the victory: "And this *schwartze?* What's he to you, exactly? He's nothing but a bum. He doesn't even have a job. Is that what you want to be all your life, a bum? I thought a doctor you wanted to be, a heart specialist. I thought *sick* people you wanted to help, not a bunch of *schwartzes* over in Black Bottom. What shall I tell people, that my son who was going to be a Big Heart Specialist is downtown with the niggers—"

"O. K., Pa, that's enough!" Yasha had shouted in disgust, and started toward the car.

Papa had followed them. "—my Son the Specialist! He'll be picking nits and scratching crabs down in Black Bottom!" he cried with helpless rage as he saw Moseley take his place in the driver's seat.

"Let's go, Moses," Yasha had said, without grief now and without repentance. "We've done what we could."

"A Specialist, he'll be, 'A Specialist of the Heart!'" Papa wept, as it became clear that they were about to abandon him. As Yasha climbed into the front seat, Kalokovich picked up a brick as if to throw it at their car, but instead he smashed it into a pile of shattered glass.

Moseley started the engine, slowly, uncertainly. It was dark and they could barely see each other any more; but Yasha could see Moseley's hand gripping the steering wheel, his body hunched over as if he were trying to see into the darkness of Hastings Street. At last, almost dreamily, Moseley pressed his foot to the accelerator. "O.K.?" he asked Yasha, as if seeking final instructions. "O.K. Let's go," Yasha had said. As they pulled away from the curb Yasha had turned back to look at his father: Papa had already seized a broom like a weapon and was violently pushing away the ruins.

Yasha tried now to dial Liza several times, but apparently when she had crashed the receiver to its cradle, the phone had fallen off the hook; and, clearly, she meant to leave it there: he received only a sustained buzzing of Busyness for his repeated efforts. He tried to shrug it off as just one of Liza's inexplicable changes of mood, but there had been a degree of uncontrollable rage in her final insult that worried him: wasted passion was not Liza's style: Yasha sometimes thought even her rages were measured for their alternately lyric or coloratura effect. In fact, when he had world enough and time, he admired Liza's rages: they rarely went very far, they were mere fine flashes of fireworks, preconditioned for his admiration: or so he believed. If they were now unexpectedly to become *real* rages, then they were in more serious trouble than he had realized. For real fury was something totally destructive, a thing full of hate. He himself had experienced it, he believed, only once—the last time he and Moseley had been arrested and kept for thirty days in that filthy Southern jail. Real fury stopped short of nothing, he knew; it ended in suicide, murder, arson, rape: it lusted for the annihilation of its object even as he had lusted after the death of that brutal cop with the obsessive intensity with which one might lust after a beautiful woman. . . .

The cop had been leading him down the corridor to his cell. After a brief trial in which Moseley had dutifully sworn to tell the whole truth on a Bible perforated "COLORED" and Yasha to tell the same truth on a Bible hygienically labelled "WHITE," he had been ordered to a separate cell block.

"Why are you separating me out?" Yasha had asked of the guard who ambled beside him down the corridor, his thick figure bent at the waist like an elbow pipe.

The answer had come slowly, as if the guard were giving considerable thought to his reply: "We don't put white niggers with black," he said.

Then suddenly they had arrived at a huge iron door, not at all like what Yasha had thought of as a city jail, but rather like a bank vault. Intimidated by this frightening exterior, Yasha had nevertheless managed a weak grin and had paused at the door of the vault just long enough for the guard, perhaps, to mistake his intention. For the swollen pipe of a body had suddenly straightened out: the guard had simultaneously gripped Yasha's arm with one hand to push him into the cell and hit him over the head with the butt of his gun. At least Yasha was always convinced that the slow, deceptively indifferent guard had struck him. He had felt, though he had never seen, the sharp karate-chop blow on the back of the neck: he had taken note of himself as he slipped into darkness, his last conscious thought had been: will he kill me? Then while he lay on the floor slowly regaining consciousness, he recalled a story Moseley had told him once about two guards who had entered a black man's cell, their weapons cocked: uncertain of their intention, the black man had picked up a chair: the guards had promptly shot the man to death. "Self-defense." It was while remembering this story that he became horribly aware of his own fear and pain. His head ached blindingly, as it had years ago after the Detroit Riot; he staggered to his feet swaying with pain and nausea. He made his way toward what he thought might be a water bucket, but it turned out to be a slop bucket smelling of disinfectant. He controlled his urge to vomit; he did not want to have to sleep in that stench all night; he was sure the guard would do nothing about it. He leaned against the wall of his cell, breathing heavily through his mouth.

The need for air attracted him to four slits of light coming from a boarded-window, reinforced by vertical bars. Yasha peered through the cracks, trying to estimate the time of day. It seemed to him about dusk. Moseley had told him that if they were jailed, it would be best to remain locked up overnight, that it was never safe to be discharged after dark. He began to examine, between periods of dizziness, the metal bed which was suspended from the wall by two chains; he measured the space of the cell, which he roughly estimated to be about ten feet long, six feet wide—adequate room for one man, but without furniture except for two pails (he had found the other, which contained drinking water). Above him a small bulb emitted a yellow light; the glass was shrouded in a metal cup through whose perforations a watery mist filtered down; it was

the light of a swamp, not a room. It occurred to Yasha that the
metal brace over the bulb was there to prevent the prisoner
from smashing it and using the glass as a weapon—either against
the guard or against himself. The guard apparently did not think
civil rights prisoners ever commit suicide; for he had left Yasha
with his belt and his fountain pen, taking away only his wallet.

Nothing, then, but two buckets and a bed. He began looking
around in the gloomy miasma for a faucet or a piece of soap
or a surface to write on. But there was nothing but the bunk
with metal, cat's-cradle slats. Over this lay two thin blankets,
one for padding against the metal slats and the other to cover
himself. He sat on the edge of the bunk holding his head in
despair; his frontal lobes felt as if they had been cut in two
with an axe; his stomach felt weak and empty; he was beginning to feel a damp chill coming up from the cement floor. He
was hungry, cold, and exhausted. Above all (and afterwards it
seemed strange that it was only at this moment that it had
struck him with full force) he was furious because he could
not get out, he could not be free—not for any reason: not for
any charity of heart, reason of politics or physical emergency
short of acute appendicitis, heart attack, or other symptoms of
imminent death—and perhaps not even then . . . . With the
disappearance of that ghoul of a guard, who clearly detested
Yasha more than he could have hated any black man, had disappeared his last contact with the outside world. What Yasha
suddenly longed for, with an inexorable urgency which rose
to his throat like a death rattle, was to get the hell out of there:
to be free. He wanted, suddenly, fresh air, sunlight, the sound
of voices in a cafe, even the wailing and weeping of women.
He wanted to lay his head on Liza's breast and hold her, hold
her, dissolve his flesh into hers to prove that he was alive. He
didn't want to die in this stinking hole. The thought that he
might do so made the hate rise to his gorge like lava; he felt
burned to a bright living ash with a hate which would never
go away; he would become a Pompeiian memorial to hate, a
passion more blinding than pain. This hate in his heart, like
the pain in his head, seemed to be something that would never

stop growing; the heat of it would consume his brains to ash. He was a crematorium of hate.

And the humiliation. Never had he experienced such shame as at this total deprivation of his free will. Not even in the tb sanatorium where he had spent the entire Second World War healing up a hole in his lung; for even in the sanatorium he had had the freedom to go home and die if he made that choice. But here, they could burn him, drown him, lynch him, shoot him, castrate him, bury him in a marshy grave, and he could do absolutely nothing. He could disappear without a trace.

Yasha's whole world had given way. Far from forgiving the guard because he knew not what he did, Yasha found him *un*-forgivable, precisely because of that ignorance which destroys. What?—forgive the beast that tore at one's throat because it knew nothing of pity? From the depths of an Intelligence which had made him a man and not an animal, that Intelligence which was to him synonymous with the soul and the hereafter, or even what one called God—Yasha was intensely aware that he hated "them": the Order of the Brute.

Afterwards, during the remainder of that trip he had been unable to explain to Moseley who "they" were; he could not distinguish vice from vice, ignorance from sadism. When he saw hate on the faces of the white hoodlums who surrounded them at bus terminals, when he saw that if they could—and they obviously wanted to—they would have crushed him beneath their feet like a roach, he felt again that surge of violent hate. While it was Yasha's conviction that pacifism was the only way for mankind to survive, his spirit had rocked with hate and destruction as the more natural medium. . . .

"Liza, where the hell did you go? I've been trying to get you for the past half hour. What's the idea of hanging up like that? That's damned childish. Two can play at that game. How'd *you* feel if I suddenly crashed the receiver down in your ear and went off to . . . went off to? . . . "

"Went off to where? To shoot buffalo? I've been sitting right here for the past half hour painting my toe nails: *white.* White as lice."

"Oh come off it. Quit the race war for a minute and tell me. What are your plans for tonight?"

She sighed as if surrendering her hate for a moment. At home she sometimes pretended he was taking her against her will, only to swallow him up in a passion that was—not unexpected, but always somehow surprising, as he might be surprised to find tears in his eyes each time Ophelia drowned. He knew, after all, the outcome of the play: the pleasure was in the performance. There was something of this involuntary caress in her voice when Liza added: "I done tole you, honey-baby. We got chicken creole with biscuits just like the little ole motherfuckin mammies used to make down in Alabam' . . . . So come on home," she added abruptly, dropping her Southern accent. It always amazed him how both she and Moseley could turn it on or off at will; they knew the music and could rephrase it when they liked. Liza used it alternately to proclaim herself the most loving and tender and dedicated of women, and to parody herself as a slave of the white master. He never questioned these mercurial transitions, figuring they were a kind of safety valve in her ambivalence toward him: their love was a double-edge sword, cutting them each time they reached out to it.

"I'm coming home," he said. "I've been trying to come home for the past hour. Why do you think I put up with being treated like a damned redneck, if I didn't expect to get home in a few minutes and make you sorry for that bitchy tongue of yours?"

Her voice had changed again: "Yasha, am I a bitch? Really? Truly? What *is* a bitch, exactly? Just intellectually, I'd just sort of like to have a definition. I've heard that used before and I can't quite figure it: a woman's a bitch in heat, a man's a son of a bitch. People say with surprise: 'Well, ain't that a bitch!' And when they want to sell a brace of pups, they say one bitch, one stud. If I'm a bitch are you just one helluva hot stud? . . . . "

"Just *intellectually* you'd just sort of like to know," he mimicked her. Sometimes I wonder why I love you, there's not an honest statement in your whole repertoire. . . . "

*Silence.* He'd gone too far. He wasn't supposed to distinguish the real from the unreal.

"And whose fault is that?" she said. Her inflection was cool and precise as a Yankee school-teacher. "Who taught us lies? Who taught us how to shuffle and squirm? If I don't know any Self except an exaggeration of my very own self so that I hardly know *who* I am: who did that to me? . . . " She waited as if expecting an answer. But she did not hang up again. For that he was grateful.

"Honey, I'm sorry. Let's just stop cutting each other up. Look, I'm just leaving the office—I'll be home in twenty minutes," he promised.

He was not able to keep his promise, however, because Moseley arrived just as he was locking up the office.

"Why you sonofabitch," cried Yasha with delight. "Why didn't you tell me you were coming in? I could have met you at the airport."

They neither shook hands, nor slapped shoulders, they had known each other too long for that; Moseley simply eased himself into a leather chair in Yasha's outer office, as though he had been sitting there for hours chatting with him about the Montgomery boycott. He now shook his head and gave Yasha a wry, affectionate glance. "Boy, I'm exhausted. My head's splitting, and I got to go out to Grosse Pointe at *once* to get us some bail money. You got an aspirin?

"Listen, what was the idea of writing me that crummy letter?"

Moseley chewed gingerly on the aspirin. Yasha watched him slowly dissolve the aspirin under his molars, then sluice it down with the water. Once in the deep South a gang of white teen-agers had forced salt petre down Moseley's throat as a Hallowe'en stunt. Though Moseley laughed it off now, claiming he was glad they had chosen *that* way to soften up his balls, he had never since then been able to swallow pills without dissolving them first. Remembering this, Yasha's tone softened: "You know damn well what you meant to do with a letter like that. I never thought you'd preach me a sermon, Moses, like that."

Moseley waved a rhetorical hand. "You know me: I gotta

preach. Just a born-black-Messiah." He sighed, looking around
Yasha's office. "Got a new painting, I see," he said disingenu-
ously. "New carpeting too."

"Yeah," said Yasha with involuntary bitterness. "That's
me: Living high. Sold out to the system. Go on. Tell me my
sins. Isn't that what a friend is *for?*"

Moseley took another swallow. "I shall forgive my friend
seventy times seven. Can I use your phone?"

"No," said Yasha curtly. "Like I let every sonofabitch comes
in here use my phone? . . . "

Moseley's fatigue and headache seemed suddenly to have
vanished; Yasha watched him admiringly as he sat on the desk:
Woodrow Moseley Williams dialing, Woodrow Moseley Williams using all his faculties at once. As he dialed with his right
hand, the receiver nestled between his shoulder and ear, with
his other he fished in his pocket for a cigarette (Yasha
frowned; he was a Puritan about smoking, hated to see his
friends burn out their lungs: a hangover from his own time
in the Sanatorium, he supposed); so he gestured his refusal to
give Moseley a light. Moseley only shrugged, grinning, turning
to the mouthpiece:

"Room 318, please. Listen, . . . I got this project out in
Grosse Pointe; seems a winner. A sure check for the Movement.
But she wants to see us personally. So call her up and make an
appointment. *Before* I get there. You break the ice . . . . "
Moseley laughed, his usually tense mouth breaking into a wide
conspiratorial smile. "Be sure to explain that the money's going
to uphold religion and the blue laws in Alabama." He glanced
at Yasha as if to share his remarks. "Listen, I got to split. I'm
with a friend: Yasha. You've met him. Yasha Kalokovich. How
many damned Yashas do you know? Oh, he might come along
down with us next time." Here Moseley nodded persuasively at
Yasha who replied with an exaggerated scowl. "O.K. See you.
Well, that's the way the cookie crumbles. . . . " Then he hung
up abruptly and sat staring at Yasha: solemn, priestly.

Yasha began to put on his coat, applying himself zealously
to the row of buttons; he stood staring back, defiantly, knowing
well what Moseley was out to do.

"You're putting on weight," said Moseley. "And I see you got some new glasses."

"Who? Me?" Involuntarily Yasha sucked in his breath, adjusted his glasses. "Use them only when I'm at the microscope."

Moseley laughed, as if with certain victory. "That's right—we only get fat and old while we *live*. Now I never feel old except . . . well 'cept when I'm in church praying old Martin Luther King won't be bombed straight to hell, or when I'm out fund-raising—like right now," he added with a glance at the clock. "Or when I'm making love to a woman. Then do I feel ainn-c--ient. . . . . Sex, religion and money you might say are the only areas in which I show my age. Otherwise I'm just a teeny-bopper."

Yasha smiled. For a moment they stood looking at one another, experimentally, cautiously, as if taking in the differences that Moseley's absence had made. It was a silence of deep trust. Their friendship had grown from the aftermath of the Great Depression, had survived a war and even Yasha's long tb bout had not prevailed against it. But what Moseley wanted of him now seemed another matter. After what appeared to Yasha in retrospect, an impossible struggle, he had only a few years ago managed to become a practicing physician. For the first time in his life he had a bit of economic security, a kind of joy in painlessness at least. When he and Moseley had met for the first time Moseley had been one of the millions of unemployed kids roaming the country looking for work. He, Yasha, had just managed to get his first job—lying about his age, of course: he had been the youngest valedictorian ever to graduate from Northern High. . . .

"Well," Moseley said peremptorily, as if not to allow him time for sentimental reminiscence. "What do you think? Coming on down with me? How you feel?"

"Well . . . different, to say the least."

"What you mean, different? You seem the same to me. 'Course, we all got to pick up our courage now and then, and *strum* on it like a guitar. Makin' freedom is an *art* and lots harder 'n picking cherries in California, I can tell *you*."

Yasha grinned as he remembered the story of Moseley's

exodus from Alabama to New York and California—the story
that had won himself and his sister Anna over the day Moseley
had shown up in the government office where Anna was employed.

. . . "Still, I suspect you the same person, after all. Spite
all this here trash you got in your office: this air-conditioning
shit and all that . . . " He cast Yasha a slew-eyed look of wisdom,
mischief, love . . .

But how could he be the same? He had been an ignorant
child the day Moseley had walked into the government office
for reallocating the unemployed—the office where his older
sister, Anna, had finally found a job. He had been such a child
that he had not realized what a coup it was for his sister to
have got a job at all at a time when there were still thirteen
million unemployed. In fact, he, Yasha, had been complaining
bitterly all this winter because every afternoon Mama would
send him to the government employment office to wait for
Anna so that she would not have to walk home alone in the
dark. Darkness had seemed to come earlier than ever this winter, and his mother had feared some sudden, brutal retaliation
from one of those numberless unhappy people whom Anna
interviewed.

On that particular November evening toward five—it had
been a bitterly cold day, he remembered, and he, Yasha, already plagued with the first of that endless succession of colds
which was to end in his long illness—had been sitting morose,
feverish and bored in the government office. His gaze rested
cynically on a sign above his sister's head: DETROIT WORK-
ERS: REMEMBER EVERY PROJECT MUST HAVE IN-
TEGRITY, BOTH IN ITS PURPOSE AND IN ITS RESULT.
Integrity bullshit. His sister had been hired as a stenographer,
but it had taken the Chief Social Worker no time at all to see
that she could do interviews better than they could, with their
ten years' experience with the Depression (it was supposed to
be nearly over, people said, now that they were on the brink of
war). Yasha watched his sister fill out her form in triplicate,
while comforting "old" men of forty, their faces cracked with

illness or fear who seemed to know just when to turn their heads piteously and say: "I've tried everything, Miss Kalokovich. I've tried everywhere. I been to L.A. and back, riding the coal cars, gondolas all the way—in the sun, in the rain." Slowly his sister would pull out her interviewing materials—application forms, wage scales, standard of living tables—she was never able to refuse anybody and the rest of the social workers regarded her as a private plague, a ratebuster . . .

Just before five, when at last all the petitioners had gone, a very young-looking black boy had strolled in. He was wearing overalls, a blue denim shirt and strange-looking brown and white shoes with perforated surfaces like fish nets. His skin was the color of strong tea, his hair a lamb's wool skull cap; his eyes reflected orbs of light, like the river. His full lips closed with difficulty over his teeth which gave him an involuntarily pleasant look, as if he were about to smile. To overcome this anomaly he hardly smiled at all, although it was a clear necessity to be pleasant to the white social worker who could decide his fate. Yasha heard him explain to his sister that he was "jes' passin through" and needed "a bit of change, so's he could go on," his sugar-sweet accent seemingly some caricature of the sharply assimilated profile. The boy stood by his sister's desk with a certain official manner, as if well trained in certain forms of deference.

"Please sit down," Anna said.

The boy took a seat precisely at a right angle to the desk, facing Yasha. The full view of his face was curious in its planes and slants; the cheekbones were high. Anna drew out one of her long yellow triplicate forms and Yasha sighed, glancing at the clock warningly. It was close to five.

"Name?" Anna asked.

"Woodrow Moseley Williams. My friends call me Moses."

His sister-the-social worker, had smiled. "Why do they call you that?"

The black boy straightened in his seat as if he were about to make a statement; then, evidently recollecting himself, he imitated a soft, soundless laugh of self-deprecation, hiding his mouth behind his hand. The palms were white as bandages, tinged pink with blood.

" 'Cause I aim to he'p my people *go*, I reckon. . . . "

"Age?" He looked about twelve or thirteen; it was a routine question. Under sixteen and they were immediately shipped home.

"Sixteen," he said promptly.

At this obvious lie his sister had not even blinked her incredulity.

"Place of birth?"

"Birmin'ham, Alabama."

"Well, you're a long way from home," observed his sister and had glanced at Yasha, indicating she was helpless in this situation; sometimes one had to work overtime. As to the distance the boy had come she made no comment: she had interviewed boys from as far as Alaska, Key West and San Diego. If Moseley had said he was from Hawaii and had swum the Pacific Ocean, his sister would have written down: "address unverifiable."

"Yes'm. Hitchhiked all the way from Memphis. Sure got hot. . . . Like to have got killed more'n once too—them crazy truckers. . . . "

As Anna remained silent, not understanding, Moseley explained: "One of them rolled me and throwed me in a ditch . . . "

"Why, what money could he have hoped to get?"

Moseley had glanced toward him before replying: "Wahn't my money."

"Oh!" Anna exclaimed with a frown. Was the boy gulling her? "Previous experience," she asked with a new air of efficiency.

"Work experience?" Moseley's eyes dilated slightly, as though reflecting on the meaning of her words. Then, as if deciding to avoid obscenities, he rolled off quickly: "Diggin. Hoein. Cottonpickin." Adding with sly bitterness: "What else a 'colored' boy like me be doin? . . . Truth is, *m'am*," he emphasized the word as if it were a white picket fence swinging him in and out: "Ah done verra little *real* work in my life. Ah'se jes' a lazy shif'less nigger. Ah jes' he'p the white massah in the fiel'."

Plainly a put-on! Yasha stood up with a forgiving smile.

His sister looked at Moseley ruefully. "Well," she said, bowing her head with humiliation: "you are a case! . . . Why'd you put on that act?"

Moseley imitated himself, laughing silently to show her his dramatic abilities; then sobering, he had explained in parable, not yet trusting them:

"You-all know what a chameleon is? Well, that's me. That's a southern black boy learning how to live in a green world, a white world, a brown world, maybe some day a black world . . . When the chameleon's out on that there mimosa tree, he's green as a baby grasshopper, but when he climbs out into the world of the true hard bark, he's pure brown. Now suppose you took the American Chameleon to Africa, to Asia, to India— what color would he be?"

Yasha stared, fascinated by Moseley's style. His sister added encouragingly: "I'm not at all sure I understand you—Moses."

"Thass' right, thass' right," Moseley affected to chortle, shaking his head and arms back and forth pendulum-wise, like a soft-shoe dancer finishing off his routine. "I'm gonna bring my people out o' bondage. I'm gonna bring em across the Red Sea *into* the lan' of 'milk an' honey—"

"Oh for Christ sake, cut the clowning and let's all get out of here!" Yasha had exclaimed abruptly. So Anna had quickly put away her devices for the Systemic Invasion of Privacy as she called them, and with a kind of conspiratorial gayety, they had all escaped from the government office. They slipped into a nearby coffee shop where you could still get coffee and dough-nuts for a dime.

"But what in God's name are you doing in Detroit?" Yasha asked as soon as they were alone. "Things are just as bad here as in Birmingham, maybe worse. Factories are just beginning to make a few planes. . . . And at least down there you can keep warm—

"Don't know where you Yankees ever got the notion there's no snow down South. It gets *cold* down there, and we've got no insulation. Wind just comes howling under the house-props. But, fact is, I haven't been home in two years."

"What've you been doing?"

"Just wandering. Thinking. Learning too. Working a day here, there, or even an hour or two for whatever they give me. ..." He paused, measuring them with his eyes. "I remember once I was on the train riding past a place near Mobile, where some prisoners were working on a private farm—the state of Alabama *rents* these prisoners out to plantation owners, guess you know that?" Moseley raised his eyes dubiously, as if he doubted, since they were white Yankees, they could know anything. . . . "Right there in the field these slaves were resting from their stoop work, just like it was still four hundred years ago: only instead of an overseer with a whip they had two guys in khaki pants and gray flannel shirts, both with rifles cocked in their arm, watching to see nobody ran away . . . The prisoners were eating, sitting down right in the swampy sidelands with their lard bucket of cowpeas and hardtack, and I yelled to one of them as our freight went shagging by: 'Hey, boss, you eat regular, don't you? I ain't had nuthin' since sun-up!' And that lifer threw me a piece of his hardtack, right into my gondola. . . . So, like I say, there's always somebody. Only don't ask anybody white *or* black who's just bought something and is making Payments. These people, they'll give you a lecture. Sloth, they'll tell you is one of the seven deadly sins: how about that? *Sloth*." And this time he showed the heart-shaped part of his lips as he laughed.

"Now why did I tell you that story?" he asked of them with a quizzical look, and in spite of themselves they had all laughed like kids on a holiday.

"Then one day the train stopped at New York," Moseley said and sighed longingly like a homesick man. He looked at Anna and Yasha with recollected delight: "That New York was something *else*! After you've been pushed around in every bus station between Jackson and Cairo, New York is just the *Book of Revelations* for a soul-seeking black man like me . . . "

Anna remarked bitterly: "Yeah—seven million people on the same subway, all trying to get the same job paying fifteen dollars a week. . . . "

"Well, things are bad in Harlem. Guess everybody knows that . . . But you know—but I guess you just *can't* know—what it was like, come night time, not to have to stay in 'niggertown.' I could go anyplace I pleased so long as I looked decent (if you were *too* dirty, a cop might pick you up, especially on the upper East Side—but that was to keep people from getting burgled, it was not necessarily something against your skin, *personally*. You understand?)." He looked at them uncertainly: "Well, look—for instance, my first day in New York, I was trying to get to my cousin's place, according to somebody else's directions and I took the wrong subway. Instead of getting off at Harlem I got off at the *white* man's side of the city . . . But the point was, nobody arrested me. Nobody started screaming 'rape.' I just walked back down into the subway and corrected my mistake . . . "

"But what did you do in New York—I mean after you figured out the subway system?" Yasha asked.

"You want to know? Well, for the first time since I got out of Birmingham, I *lived*. . . . . If you ask me what I lived on, I can't rightly say. Sometimes it was stuff I cooked for myself in a big pot, and sometimes it was stuff I got hanging around outside the kitchen at Longchamps (there were still people in the world who didn't eat up every damned thing on their plate, would you believe it?). I never did do any real garbage-eating. . . . "

"Nor did I," interposed Anna suddenly, to Yasha's surprise. "But I've seen them. I saw them while I was visiting my Uncle in Chicago . . . The men came carrying it in fresh barrels . . . and kids would fish around with sticks . . . I was only a kid myself—but it made me sick. I've never forgotten it. I guess that's why I'm still in Detroit." At the sight of Anna's youthful face already empty of hope Yasha felt a bitter pang of inexplicable guilt, as though he were somehow responsible—he, the late-in-life baby who had wrecked Mama's health and somehow forced his sister too early into the world of work. "I guess that really scared me," his sister added. "At least here—" she looked around her uncertainly, "I felt I wouldn't starve . . . At least here I knew people . . . " Her voice faltered.

"Now: ain't that the truth!" Moseley exclaimed—grotesquely dialectal, ignoring the personal complaint in Anna's remarks as if it were a deprivation beyond recompense. "But a tight gut can give you plenty of know-how, believe you me," he added sharply. "Like the wolf versus the house-dog in the fable: at least you don't have the mark of the collar on you, do you, Wolfie?" he addressed some unknown person who was hungry-but-free, presumably himself. He laughed. "I went to the New York Public Library, and I got me some books: Bernard Shaw, H. G. Wells, Bertrand Russell. I fixed up an old radio dumped in the trash and I listened to WQXR . . . I listened to black artists for the first time—*my* people, black people doing big things—*respected*, and I began to be ashamed that my ole great-grand-pappy was as white as you are. I began wishing I were *all* black, and that never happened to any 'Bama nigra that I know, suh.

"I found me a little room at the top of nowhere with another black boy. I learned about a whole lot of things . . . Man, we had talks like we'd just invented speech. This pal of mine, he was a *black* man from Barbados. And he had a new word, *negritude*. . . ." He paused, evidently considering whether his roommate's discoveries might not be of limited interest for his white audience. Then allowed his style to shamble back to that of the blithe adventurer: "And so I hit the road one day when it was snowin a pack of white friskies. *Mush!* I said, and started for California. . . .

"Ever been there?"

Yasha shook his head, feeling very young, and inexplicably ashamed of his innocence, as though innocence in these bad days were the ultimate culpability.

"I could write a book about California," said Moseley. "Only one thing I'll say right now 'cause I know you-all have to go on home. Like you got a Mama worries about you, where you at and all that. Don't knock it! I sure wish I had somebody worryin' about *me* . . . .

"California," he went on, "is America *par excellence*. Is that right? Is that the way you say it?" he asked Anna in an aside; Anna shrugged and he went on: "That's where you see it the *most*. That's where the most beautiful grapes in the world hang on the sweetest vines: but time you get to em, they're all sour: get me?

"California," he said, "is the reverse of the South: in the South, you're in a hell bending down—stoop work. In California, you're in a hell stretching up—shoulder work." He was becoming excited. "This is what I mean. . . . It takes you from Christmas, say, to nearly springtime to hitchhike and work-hike your way three thousand miles, and finally you get to cross over from Nevada into Lake Tahoe. . . . Let's *suppose* now, let's just imagine, that you are the luckiest SOB migrant worker in the *en*tire four hundred miles of orchards up and down California. Let's us just imagine that they didn't find lice in your hair, boll-weevil in your cotton-head, anthrax or hoof and mouth disease on your poor old cow-feet, aedipus egyptus mosquitoes in your water bottle—so they don't deport you back to Nevada, and you actually get across that state line into the Promised Land. And let's us imagine a miracle: say twenty laborers all just dropped dead of the heat in this little village near Stockton in the San Joaquin Valley, and the cherry trees are ripening like an epidemic—like the red hordes of China, as you might say . . . You've got a *chance* then, if you're a walking-worker. You line up at the corner of Hope and Hunger Streets, waiting for them to get you around five in the morning. And the miracle holds good. Some whole dumb family of Mexicans got the trots from eating too many cherries, and so now they need a couple plugs to plug up a manhole. . . . So me and about thirty other guys stand on the same corner, waiting to get picked up to go cherry-picking."

Moseley paused and glanced at the clock; it was nearly six and already workers with lunch buckets were coming in out of the cold to have a coffee or roll while awaiting the street car or bus that would carry them home. In his eagerness to make his point Moseley laid one hand restrainingly on Yasha as if he thought Yasha and his sister might rise to give up their places to these tired-looking men; but Yasha, spellbound by Moseley's style, his head spinning with what later turned out to be a fever of 103°, scarcely turned his head as the workers filed in.

Moseley smiled contentedly. "O. K. You got the picture?" He held out his hands, boxlike, imitating a photographer. "There

I am, standing at the corner of First and Main, Cherryville, California. No little grocery store open yet, so no breakfast . . . It's a bit chilly. The sun hasn't quite come up . . . Fact is, it might rain today, but makes *NO DIFF*, we pick cherries, rain or shine. We're going to climb up on those twenty-five foot ladders and poke a lightning bolt right back in the sky if necessary . . .

Two other black men with me. About ten Mexicans, and one poor slob all the way from Florida, and another, a big guy, a Negro-baiter already grumbling about working with a 'passle of niggers.' But I'm too dismal to worry about *those* problems. I smell coffee somewhere and I'm thinking of selling my black soul to the Devil if He'll just send me over a cup of coffee. But just about then a truck pulls up—one of those with horizontal slats on each side, like they use for shipping cattle to the freight train, y'know? We all pile in, standing up: there's no room to sit down, and besides we've got to be ready to jump off when the driver says 'Jones' orchards—three men needed. Pick you up little before dark. Unless you decide to sleep here.' . . . Now *sleep* here—that means wrapping up in your skin or blanket, whichever you have handiest, and sleeping on the ground. Only the really *big* companies supply any kind of shacks for the pickers. And as for a place to shit," he glanced at Anna. She shrugged. "There's one outhouse for everybody and you may have to walk a mile to get to it: you lose time, energy . . . so even the women get used to using the fields. Well, as I say, I'm the Lucky One. They need me, Woodrow Moseley Williams, black boy, to pick purple and rose-colored cherries. Now there's something real beautiful about cherries. What's that poem about the woman who gets a bowl of cherries and the Duke is mad with jealousy because of the gift and he kills her or something? What I mean is, cherries are symbolic. Not like black-eyed peas . . . And when the trees are really *full,* they look like a clump of Heaven.

"But suppose they're not full. Suppose just last week a family of migrants went through that orchard like a blast—pushing their portable house (meaning a *car,* man) around on their backs, like turtles, and picking cherries like madmen,

they *got* most of them—except those at the very top . . . except those in tricky little clusters here and there about twenty feet up from the ground. What does a lucky nigger like me do then? Sun-up to sun-down, I move that ladder around through the tree tops. 'There's a good bunch! Get it!' yells the overseer. So I move the ladder again. And again. Till by noon I've got my first bucketful. (A bucket-*full* has got to be pyramid-shaped, cherries rolling off the center point like out of a cornucopia.) Out of what they pay me for the bucketful, the contractor—*not* the owner—knocks off a dime. The contractor is the one who just sits at a table; you show him your bucket; he counts out the change, then with a little knife—as if it's too small an amount for him to handle—he scrapes a dime off your pile back into *his* pile . . . like a goddamned croupier in a high class Reno gambling joint. One thing is good, though. You don't go hungry. You can eat your own cherries if you like . . . But dinner comes expensive that way: it's like eating your own seed crop.

"So then Ole Lucky-Moseley gets through the day, and instead of sleeping in the Ravine Motel, which is a ditch beside the orchard, I go back to Main Street in Cherryville. Here I can't decide whether to keep going to Stockton and maybe head south to L. A. or to sleep in the porch of the post office. I decide on the post office . . . In the morning I get a good shakedown by the guy who opens the P. O. but at least I'm not arrested for vagrancy. You know, one sign I'll never forget —saw it many places afterwards, but this was the first time, it was in Cullman, Alabama. Just as I was about to lie down in a ditch there, I saw this sign, as big as a billboard, in black and white letters bigger than I am. It said: 'NIGGER—Don't Let The Sun Go Down on You in This Town.' And they meant it. . . . "

Yasha and Anna sat in astonished silence. Moseley's manner was so droll they had naturally felt inclined to laugh; yet at the same time they had felt shock, respect, a pity which they could never have expressed.

With fantastic irrelevance Moseley leaped to his feet. "See that picture? It's Joey-baby."

They had turned to where Moseley was pointing, not with his finger but with his clenched fist, his shoulder in the curved pose of a prizefighter. On the opposite wall was a yellowing fly-specked poster of Joe Louis, Heavy-Weight Champion of the World. Moseley jabbed a right into space, purring: *"Didn't he smash that white son of a bitch though? . . . "* Then he stopped in embarrassment. Without realizing it, it was their moment of truth: Moseley had stood up, waiting for their faces to assume a look of cold, collective insult, the white man's phalanx against the black. Moseley's eyes glistened a moment: he poked at Yasha with a feigned professional jab which was not hostility at all, but restrained affection. . . . . "I saw that fight . . . Ha! Give it to em Joey-baby. Smash that white son of a bitch," he repeated. Then sobering abruptly: "Let's get out of here and let these guys sit down. They're going to be on their feet all night . . . . " At his command, Yasha and Anna had risen automatically, while Moseley watched them, assessing them with the same smile with which he now regarded Yasha: were they strong enough to follow him? his eyes had seemed to question.

As they continued to question: "No difference that I can *see*," added Moseley philosophically.

"Nobody stands still. People change. I *know* I'm different. One more bust in the head and that'll be the end of Kalokovich, M.D. Of course I can always sell newspapers. Nobody cares about environmental health anyway. . . . "

"I'm not asking you to get busted in the head. Just come down and help us. Take care of the sick. Ain't that what a doctor suppose to do? They don't need you to walk ten miles a day, but they do need somebody to ease the pain . . . "

"Before this is over, there won't be anybody who can ease all the pain. If that's all you want, you don't need a doctor to give away aspirin . . . "

Momentarily silenced, Moseley stared at the floor. "Were you fixin to go?"

"Yeah. I got to meet Liza. She's burned up about something. I never know what till it hits me."

"How things going?"

"Same. A terrific girl. I wish she'd grow up . . . "

"You mean by that you wish she'd see things your way."

Yasha methodically began looking in his pockets for things which he knew were not there. Moseley was veering to the edge of a subject he did not like, the question of marriage, families, children. . . . To avoid arguing with him on his first night home, Yasha inquired: "You think the boycott will work?"

"Yeah. It'll work. King is a power. Power is King. Whichever way you look at it, the people love him. *I* love him. They'll do anything for him. The kids would die for him. And when you got the kids you really got a Movement. Fill the jails with the kids, and the parents'll fight lions and tigers to get in with them."

"A Children's Crusade, eh? But I remember what happened to *them*."

Moseley's face became implacable. "Every year five hundred kids in Birmingham, Alabama *die* from not getting any decent food, from getting kicked around in hospitals with freaks in them instead of doctors, from what police records call 'accidents.' These are the kids from the Crusade. These are the unknown martyrs. We got to make them *known*: write songs for them, books about them, put em on TV—get all the publicity we can—"

Yasha halted the futile search through his pockets (he could no longer remember what he had been looking for anyway) and stared—visibly skeptical: "So civil rights has become Big Business. All you need is good PR men: what's good for General Motors is good for Martin Luther King, Jr. . . . "

Moseley looked as if he were trying to be patient, but Yasha knew him well enough to see that he was irritated. "Not civil rights. Human rights. I shouldn't have to tell *you* that. You're where I heard it from first. . . . "

"O. K. I know all about that. Why don't you try to remember that you're not talking to Orville Faubus? But my conviction is our first obligation is to be civilized. Sending kids into the streets to demonstrate, *hoping* they'll get arrested, *hoping* they'll be martyrs is just plain ruthlessness. It's not—civilized."

"You're wrong about this, Yasha, that's all. Just 100% wrong. You haven't been in it. You haven't seen the power a kid has over his own folks. A nine year old can shame his folks into going to jail for the sake of the kid's future. . . . Listen, you know damn well those cops down there wouldn't mind roughing up a kid no bigger than a yucca stalk—"

The medical man rose harsh, uncompromising in Yasha: "Obviously not *your* kid being carried into the emergency room looking like hashed brown potatoes. . . . I don't see how a couple of guys like us, who refuse to have kids of our own have any right to ask other people to sacrifice their children for the fucking future . . .

" . . . What future, anyway? Listen, between the bomb and the chemicals we don't *have* any future. . . . "

Moseley's eyes widened. "Something's really bugging you."

"*People* are bugging me, that's all. People who are ripping off the big round ball 'whereon I stand' . . . "

"Let's go someplace and talk." Moseley glanced around at Yasha's spotless office, with its silent corridors leading to examining rooms. "I hate doctors' offices," he said. "Let's get to hell out of here."

"Liza will freak out if I don't get there in twenty minutes like I promised."

"Well, don't tell me it's the first time you ever kept her waiting. . . . "

"First you tell me I don't treat her right, and now you want to take advantage of the fact that I'm a mean old sonofabitch to keep her waiting."

Moseley lavished his most conspiratorial smile: "Yowzah, Massah K., we got to keep the ole white conscience a'bilin' away. . . . Listen, Yasha, I got a story to tell you. You never were one to turn down a story."

"About cherry-pickers in California?"

"No: about cotton-pickers in Alabama . . . "

"Well, cut the mystery and tell me what you and your bunch of do-gooders have really been doing down there."

Moseley looked as if he would have liked to pick up the

"do-gooder" point with something trenchant, but managed to say in a slow delighted way, like a kid licking a lollypop, "We've been *walkin'* . . ."

"Walking?"

"Just walking. That little old woman, Rosa Parks, started it all. Not getting up and letting that white man have her seat. . . . Whoever said woman's place is in the home? Woman's place, man, is on the bus.

"It was beautiful," he went on after a moment, "just beautiful, that's all I can say. You should have been there to see it. You'd see these Negro women, been working for white folks all their lives—walking three, four, *ten* miles a day rather than ride the buses. They even made up a freedom song about it. . . . The song got to be a kind of church *response*, you know? A little after sunrise I might be walking along down Tallapoosa Street toward town and I'd meet one of these women in their white uniforms. Seemed like they were springing up right out of the mud gullies. They'd be wearing some torn-up old shoes for walking to work in, and under their arms, carrying their white work shoes. 'Good morning, m'am,' I'd say, 'Your feet sure look tired . . .' and they'd sing back the chorus: 'That's right, that's right—*but my soul is rested.* . . .'

"Still, after we got it together, we had seventeen thousand boycotting the buses. We got three thousand of them to work every day. . . . Car pools. We'd start real early, we had about thirty-five places for people to meet, about a hundred and fifty cars, and by nine o'clock or near to it as we could make it, we had every black worker in Montgomery on the job. . . . Yeah, that was the lucky day for the Movement, the day Rosa Parks was riding the bus: suppose she'd stayed home to bake cookies?"

"Suppose King had taken the presidency of the NAACP instead?" suggested Yasha.

Moseley nodded, clapping his hands together as if they were engaged in some ancient rhythmic rite. "That's how it was. That's how it was. The people of Montgomery had him picked for the N Double A CP but King said he was too new to the town. *Modest,* you know. Didn't want to do anything too *big!*

But that Reverend Nixon had the ministers all called together
—it was the night they planned the boycott—and Nixon said:
'Am I to tell our people that you are cowards?'" Moseley fairly
chortled at the phrase. "Martin Luther just raised his hand to
show *he* was ready to be counted. And he sure got himself a
new job that day, heading the Montgomery Improvement As-
sociation. And what I mean, it *improved*! Nearly eighteen
million blacks love him like Jesus Christ Himself."

"That doesn't give Him much more time—"

"Hmmm?"

"—till He's crucified."

"Well, that's what Jesus was all *about*. King-Jesus is nonviolent: he prays for the other guy. So they'll have to crucify
him, I guess. You should have heard him in that Baptist Church
on the night of the boycott. Fifty thousand blacks in Montgomery, and every one of them trying to get into the Baptist
Church. Like they came to hear the Emancipation Proclamation.
Nearly three thousand people, including myself, and when I
heard that Voice say 'There comes a time when people get
tired . . . *tired* . . . did you hear, I said *tired?*' I just wanted
to take up my bed and *walk*. 'Yea, Lord,' I said to myself,
'I'm coming.' Yasha—he could make you believe the white
man was just a saint with a bad smell. Have you ever read
that first article he wrote on the boycott? Well I did, after I
heard him down in Montgomery, and ever since then I feel
as if I'm being followed around by this Voice saying: 'Let us
pray that God shall give us strength to remain nonviolent
though we may face death.'"

"I hear," observed Yasha, running his hands through his
hair to touch the scar where the old stitches had been, "I hear
that the White Citizens Council is telling people to use anything
they can lay hands on—stones, slingshots, bows and arrows,
bowie knives—to abolish what they called '*black slimy juicy
unbearably stinking niggers. . . .*'"

Moseley shared a bitter smile. "Poetic, aren't they? But
it's not bows and arrows we have to worry about. It's dynamite.
Birmingham's KKK has got enough dynamite stored away to
blow us all to kingdom come . . . *King*—dom come, I mean. . . ."

Yasha shook his head. "And you want to fight that kind of thing on your knees! Jesus Christ!" Yasha raised his eyes heavenward.

"Well: before you kill a man, even a Kluxer, you got to hate him. And I don't think King hates anybody . . . I don't think he's training black kids to hate Kluxers. He's trying to awaken the *white conscience,* of America, that's what he's trying to do."

Well, *I* don't have too much trouble hating," muttered Yasha, recalling the cop in the jail.

"King's started the biggest thing that's ever happened to the black people. He's going to unite black and white . . . And how's he going to do it? With L-O-V-E, Yasha, that's all, like it says in the Good Book. *Massive* resistance, that's what we had in Montgomery. Fifty thousand blacks praying for Justice. . . . From here we can go anywhere, even get elected to office."

"— and get dynamited," said Yasha laconically.

"Who ever heard of a revolution without people getting killed?"

"What the hell kind of a pacifist leader are you, planning a revolution?"

"Yasha, I'm after the ultimate change. You don't get that without a couple of crucifixions. . . . "

"You ready?"

"Not yet," admitted Moseley. "I got work to do first."

"*You're* not expendable."

"Not yet," repeated Moseley. "We need not only messiahs, we need leaders. And we need em educated." He sat silently a moment, pushing his drink around an invisible axis with his fingertips. "Yasha, what do you think? . . . What if I decided to go back to college? There're a lot of things I don't know. Black history, for instance. I don't even know for sure how we all got to this country in the first place. . . . Do you think it's too late? To get an M.A. or something?"

"It's never too late to *get* one of their damned degrees. But it's sometimes too late to *use* it."

"What you mean?"

"Well, just look at me, for instance. I finally became Doctor

Kalokovich. After working my ass off for fifteen years, after being an imitation camp counselor, an imitation waiter, bus boy, postal clerk, personnel manager, an imitation research assistant to a very *real* shit at Wayne State, they finally let me have this diploma—" he pointed to a gold-labelled degree hung above his desk—" and let me start practicing medicine. But I still feel as ignorant as dirt. It makes me furious when I think of all those years of shitwork, when I should have been learning what I needed to know. . . . "

"You shouldn't have been wasting your time with all those high-status jobs," laughed Moseley. "You should just have got on the Ford assembly line like the rest of us! But no," he added seriously. "I don't mean to do it that way. I mean to get one of those grants they're starting to give to black people. I mean, they *need* blacks now to prove how democratic they've always been . . . Then I'll feel ready—"

"Ready for what?"

"For the 'Big Invasion.' We got this really big idea now. We're going to go South in a caravan of buses. . . . Going to test the Interstate Commerce Law, sit at restaurants, register blacks to *vote*. It's never been done before in the deep South, you know."

"You're mad. You'll get killed the minute you get south of Cairo."

Moseley touched his lips with a stern look, like a man measuring a weapon. "We got to try," he said. "We got to bust the South wide open, then work our way up, get into the *economic* thing up North, the 100% black school in Chicago, that kind of thing. . . . And I want you to come with me, Yasha. I need you. Listen, you're not going to screw around here the rest of your life with your high-yaller whore, are you?"

Yasha flushed. "Liza is *not*—" He was so angry he did not trust himself to speak.

He was so angry he did not trust himself to speak.

"Well what is she then?" Moseley demanded. "You don't want to marry her. You don't want to have kids. You waiting for the Virgin Mary to come along? So far as *us* black people is concerned she ain't *nuthin* but your high-yaller whore, just like in the good old days back on the plantation. . . "

"Moses, cut that out, will you? I love the woman. You know that." He sighed. "Would I put up with all these scenes if I didn't love her?"

"Well: *would* you?"

Yasha sighed, glanced guiltily at his watch. "Moses, you're putting me on the spot. A guy can hardly *not* go to bed with a woman he wants, especially if she wants him to . . . Yet if he doesn't hang out a sign *licensed for marriage,* then he's a bastard, a racist, a—"

"O.K. Don't explain it all to me. Make Liza see it that way. She's the one wants to marry you, not me. All I want is—"

"My life," said Yasha, and smiled, his lips parting painfully. "I'll have to think about it," he said. "My only regret is that I have but one life to lay down for racist America."

"You give me a call about that," Moseley chided him.

Yasha watched as his old friend made a tight fist around the sleeve of his sweater, then with a violent thrust pushed the black hand through the camel-colored coat.

"Grosse Pointe, here I come!" said Moseley, and marched toward the door with the same insouciance with which he had once left Yasha at the Sanatorium, when he had been on his way to the Second Great War. And which great war was this to be? Yasha wondered.

He was very late and he found Liza, as he might have expected, sitting by the fireplace in what seemed to him an elaborately prepared solitude. The door had been locked, he had been obliged to use his key; she had, he felt, pretended not to hear him groping in the dim light of the hall to find the lock. The lights of her apartment were all dimmed. Even the mirror above the artificial fireplace reflected only the rectangular glooms of modern furniture; the egg-shaped plastic chairs and formica top tables gave off no relieving shadows; the red neon coils of the fireplace offered a flickering pulse of life, but as their shadows darted in and out of the flared bones of her face they merely changed her color from creme de cacao to a deep rose.

Yasha stood in silence watching her, letting her absorb the fact that he was there—hoping to soften her anger by his silent penitence. He saw now that two bowls of soup rested on the tiled brick around the fireplace; the unused spoons glinted in the darkness. On the surface of the soup a red core of oil had hardened to a solid floe.

"I'll be ready to go in a minute," she said mechanically. It was then that he noticed she was already in evening dress and wearing one of the several blonde wigs she used on stage. This one had either been remodeled or was entirely new; for it was a bright silver-blonde shade, willfully artificial. Clearly she had dressed for "on stage" so that she could wait until the last possible moment for him. She now glanced with indifference at the star-shaped clock which extended the Roman radii of its hands into an otherwise naked wall. Liza claimed she did not like to clutter her walls with paintings but Yasha believed it was because when she had first moved in with him his apartment had been lined like a gallery with prints and paintings. Liza pretended not to "understand" art and insisted on keeping their place as different as possible from Yasha's "old bachelor's quarters," as she called them.

"Actually, Gussie is doing a long solo tonight," she explained as if they were continuing their telephone conversation. "He's good for twenty minutes, at least."

"I could drive you over." He was hesitant, uncertain what her intention could be in delaying their departure, since it was clearly too late for them to have dinner together.

With a great effort, as if she were afraid of shaking herself, Liza moved from where she had been sitting on the floor into an armchair; then she sat with her hand on her chest, breathing deeply.

He was puzzled, but not alarmed. He knew Liza to be in superb health; she had never had any physical complaints and always appeared radiant with energy. After years of hunger and terror in her Alabama childhood, she was eager for life; she claimed she had no time to be ill, and was always ready to be turned on to anything new and exciting. Now she sat in the chair, tilted and rigid as a matchstick in a cup.

"Have your dinner?"

"No, not yet. I thought I'd wait till after the show, then we can go out some place to eat." He threw off his coat and made an empty gesture of warming his hands a moment at the artificial fireplace.

"Rather not."

"Liza, I'm sorry. You know I didn't mean a thing by what I said."

"Oh, *that*." Her tone let it all fall away into the remote past.

"You ought to know that for us, at least—"

She raised her head attentively.

"—stupid questions of race don't exist."

"You mean that? . . . I mean, you believe you mean that, don't you?"

"Well, for God's sake, Liza. If I *say* it, I mean it. Besides, if I've got to explain how I feel—"

"—yes, explain how you feel . . . " It was not a plaintive echo, but a challenge.

"I don't understand all this. Why this sudden militancy? You a black nationalist or something all of a sudden?" He hoped the absurdity of the question would bring a faint smile, at least; but she merely flicked her eyes irritably, as if she had no time for questions asked merely for private diversion.

"Maybe I am. Who knows? . . . Gussie is no fool, and he says all white men are devils."

"And you agree with him, I suppose?" He thought his voice managed to sound heavily ironic.

"Sometimes. . . . "

What puzzled him was her strangely undramatic way of speaking, an emotionless sincerity; she made it plain that there was no one present whom she cared to charm with either her fake Oxonian or 'quaint' Alabama speech. In her very absence of accent lay the seriousness of judgment: he felt himself the object of it.

"Fine turn of events," he affected to grumble, delaying the verdict, though eventually he was certain he must be declared innocent. "—a man comes home to his woman and she calls him a Devil. . . . "

"*I* didn't call you that. I said Gussie, or Minister Ibn X as he calls himself, says *all* white men are devils. I heard him say so . . . at the Mosque."

"My God, Liza, you're not serious. You haven't really been going to listen to those fanatics."

"'Fanatics?'" she echoed challengingly; but he did not take up the cudgel. Then after a moment, she admitted: "No . . . I've only been once. But he's given me something to think about."

"So that's what's been eating you lately. You've fallen for that crazy theory about who got to the Garden of Eden first— Adam or W. H. Fard. . . . . "

"No . . . "

"What then?" he demanded, with more ferocity than he had intended.

She was silent.

"Is it Gussie?"

Her spear-shaped yellow pupils bore into his; then she looked into the fire, shrugging contemptuously.

"Is it . . . Do you have some idea, some notion, that some *woman?* . . . " He resented the fact that she had succeeded in making him sound like a fatuous ass.

"What do you mean?"

Her air of innocence exasperated him. "Oh dammit! I know you *always* think I'm hot for every woman who comes to my office."

"*Are* you?" She bit down on the words like a bullet.

"I'm not even going to deign to answer such a silly question. Now will you turn this show off and let's go? I can take some work along and wait for you. We'll eat at the ten o'clock break."

"I'm not hungry."

"Well, you've got to eat something," he said mechanically.

"Food sickens me."

He stared.

She turned a sidelong, almost malicious smile in his direction. "I've been sick three mornings . . . "

He refused to believe it. She was playing some new game with him, getting carried away with her role.

"—and what I *crave* more than anything in the world is a cup of sassafrass tea. . . . "

"You're not pregnant," he announced, but it was a question.

For a moment the Liza he loved revived; she giggled: "Fine doctor you are—can't tell a pregnant woman from a spayed cat!"

"But you can't be pregnant. Those pills have been tested. They're reliable. They've been tested . . . " he repeated. "They're fool-proof."

"Ah, *fool*-proof!" she exclaimed with a stifled gasp, almost of triumph.

"—and you're no fool," he added bitterly. "So what happened?"

"Guess I forgot to take em—or take one. . . . "

"*Forgot!* How could you forget something like that. It's like forgetting to breathe. You must have *wanted* to forget."

She flared. "What do you mean, *wanted?*"

"For Chrissake, Liza, tell me the truth. Did you take your pill as I instructed?"

" '*Instructed*'?" She raised her brows contemptuously. "Reckon you cain't learn a nigger *nuthin.*"

"Cut the comics, and tell me."

"Tell you what?"

"Did you or did you not *omit* taking your pills?"

She was silent.

He drew a deep breath. "Liza, you can't have this baby!"

She bridled, shot him a malevolent look. "What makes you think I can't? You just watch."

"I'm not watching. I'm doing." He walked to the phone and flicked through the directory a moment. "You're mad, Liza," he said, turning to her again as he tried to dial the number and received a busy signal.

"No use calling any of your white witch doctors," she announced. "I'm not going to him." Then with a sudden spurt of rage she sprang up from the armchair and began pulling on her shoes; with silent rage she shoved the pillows back in place, gathered up the untouched bowls of gumbo, and with methodical fury carried them into the kitchen and hurled them into the sink, smashing every dish. "Just as low as Ibn X says they are," she said. "All they want is to sleep with you. They don't want any kids, any home—they just want to pay and go. They make whores of us all—just like Ibn X says they do."

He put down the phone. "Liza, come here and stop all that nonsense. What the hell is Gussie or Ibn X or whatever he calls himself now, to you and me?"

"Don't couple yourself with *me*, White-man. I didn't believe him: I said to Ibn X, 'If it's his child, he'll be so happy. He doesn't even know how happy it's going to make him. And it'll be so light . . . it won't be any problem at all. . . . Just like his Daddy,' I said. Simple as . . . simple as black and white . . ." She stood staring at him, not moving from the sink where the shards of gumbo lay in colored fragments.

"Let's sit down and talk this over like two civilized people."

"*I'm* civilized," she exclaimed hotly. "But I don't know about you!"

He looked at her with what he hoped was medical detachment. "You're not going to go into a *sturm und drang* about 'murdering an unborn child' are you?"

A faint smile lurked at the corners of her mouth; it was a smile almost of triumph, as if she now knew something he didn't. "Ah, a good strong expression. When one resorts to murder, it's always good to have strong expressions, like *lebensraum, nach dass ostend, anchschluss* . . . Though, of course, to destroy a *schwein-hund* of a black child would not be murder in any case."

"Liza, listen to reason and stop making false analogies. You can't have this child. I have something to say about it, don't I? The child is mine, isn't it?"

Her eyes froze, turned to craters of broken glass: "What the hell do *you* think?"

He took her hand in his. "All the more reason to listen to me. I know better than you about these things. In the first place, a child, any child, needs a father—"

"Well?"

"But even more than a father he needs a world he can survive in. And what kind of a world do we have to offer? . . . A world of radioactive fall-out, of thousands starving to death every day of the year . . . Is that a world to bring a child into? . . . Dammit, if you want a kid, adopt some orphan—there were plenty of them born during the war. But don't ask me to call him mine. I don't want to be anybody's father. Besides, I'm not such a healthy guy any more, you know that . . . " He faltered. He always avoided talking about his health, his years in the Sanatorium, his collapsed lung, as any emphasis on the physical was apt to point up the differences in their ages: a kind of taboo castration-reference, he thought grimly.

"Liza, I'm only asking you to do this for your own good—for the child's good. The operation is nothing—it's over in twenty minutes. Under sterile medical conditions it's perfectly safe."

"Words, man, words. This here's a baby you're talking about, not a specimen under your damned microscope. Why don't you just tell the truth and admit you don't want any truck with a nigger woman's baby—just like all the white Bosses?"

"It's not true and you know it. Besides the child would be 'white' or 'almost white,' whatever that means."

"Try *pure* white like the TV commercials say," she put in bitterly.

He ignored her; he felt he had a point to make which explained it all: "I don't want to be responsible for any child's unhappiness—or even his happiness—"

"You don't want to be responsible for anything!" she snapped. "You don't figure you owe this baby his chance?"

He slapped his brow. "Why did you do it?" he demanded. "Did you want to test my goddam love or something? Does love have to be tested?"

" 'Tested. . . . Strengthened.' What does that mean? If people live together long enough, sooner or later they think about having a baby: they decide for or against."

"But you didn't let me decide."

She hesitated. "No. Because I was afraid you'd say no. But I never realized you thought so little of me you'd chop me through with one of those axes they use to kill off little black babies."

"A *curette*, dammit, is not an axe—above all not in the hands of a professional. And it's not a little black child. It's nothing at all yet. It's just a blob."

"No such thing as a blob. Out of a blob heaven and earth were created. God is a blob."

"God is dead, like the rest of heaven—and someday, probably, earth."

"You really believe that?"

"I'm not sure. . . . But He's not dead, He's hard of hearing. For a God, that amounts to the same thing. It's a 100% disability. Liza, you're not going to have this baby."

"*Am.*"

"Over my dead body. . . . "

"No, Suh. In mah *live* one, Boss."

"If you don't cut out that Boss-stuff, I swear I'll—"

"You'll what, chicken-heart?"

"O.K. Call me names. Only don't call on me to be the father of this child. I won't recognize it. I won't do a damned thing for it. I won't even stay here for him to be born." He hoped, fiercely, that he was intimidating her, that she believed him.

"Running out?" she said coldly.

He nodded, steeling himself in order to be kind; he refused to be caught in that three-fold cord—of frailty, love . . . and guilt. He had seen it too often: sound-minded men reduced to mammering idiots, trapped in the sweet nectar of immortality. "I'll make an appointment for you," he said. "I know a doctor."

"Oh you smart ones. You always know a doctor. You-all so well *instructed*. Tell me, does this doctor have a tattooed number on his arm, or is he one of your own—of the super-race?"

"You really believe it. You really believe that it's because I'm white and you're black"—he formed quotations around the words with his index fingers—"that I don't want this baby."

She stood at the threshold, waiting for him to go. "No," she said. "It's because you're a goddamned *Devil* and I'm *black*."

"For Chrissake. You're no more black than I am!"

"Aah! . . . " She stood leaning against the door a moment.

Then after a long silence she added: "My heart is black. You can't change that."

"Liza," he said suddenly, "if you'll give up this insane notion of having a baby—" he took a deep breath, conquering himself, as it were, by surprise, "—we'll get married."

She smiled, however, as if it were no surprise to her: "That's quite a bribe, Herr Doktor. Now take me to the 'showers.'"

Her attitude made him furious. It seemed to him that his offer of marriage was as far as he could go to make her 'happy.' He refused to father alienated children to suffer in a rotting society. "Dammit!" he exploded, bringing his fist with rage into his left hand. "Do you know what the hell you *want?*"

At the very real rage in his voice, Liza crumpled. She began to cry silently, not as he would have imagined, but beginning with a loud wail like a traditional lament at a funeral pyre. Then she sank to the floor and gave herself up to great shafts of grief that rushed through her throat with the sharp crushing sound of boots in a thicket. Tears charred her face, leaving dark trails through the rose-tint powder.

He knelt beside her. "Please stop. Stop it. Liza. Stop. I can't stand it to listen to you. What do you want? I've told you I love you, isn't that enough? That I'll marry you, even—" the intensifier flicked involuntarily across his dry lips.

"I wanted you to love this baby. Just to love this baby."

Yasha did not reply; he rose from his knees.

For a while Liza sat sobbing, with slow shuddering sighs, rhythmic and resigned; then she too rose, went to the bathroom, applied a heavy layer of powder around her eyes, and left for work.

Yasha did not offer to drive her.

"You can wait here," said the nurse as she leaned against the slatted door adjoining the two rooms. Yasha noticed her muscled forearm, under which she had tucked two folded, fresh sheets: the tight white sleeves of her uniform made a knifelike ridge in her flesh. "That way, if we need you . . . for any reason, we can call you. Also—" she pointed with the rounded bulwark of her shoulder, "as you go out, there's an exit to the left. You probably saw it?"

Yasha shook his head; he had seen nothing. He had been too busy trying to break through Liza's silent fury; but whenever he thought he had touched her heart with some little tenderness or pathetic joke, she had suddenly flicked out at him a scorpion sting of rage and withdrawn into brooding silence.

The nurse turned her mountainous bulk on him while she made a show of not locking the door of the room behind which Liza lay, waiting.

"Nothing to worry about," she assured him in a hearty voice. "I've seen em before. They're always nervous." She smiled at him; her smile was terrifying. Between two bulging pouches of cheek lay a pair of eyes like pitch; sideburns harassed her jowls. Yasha looked away as with a thrust of her muscular forearm she signalled to Liza not to get up from the table.

"I'm Mrs. Sledge," Yasha heard her say as the door shut on the two women. The fact that she was married astonished him: who would marry that giant troll with tufts sprouting from her chin? He decided he was just badly shaken up, getting Kafkaesque about it all. The nurse was neither giant nor troll; she was suffering from a glut of androgyns, that was all.

He had thought that, when the time came, he would be perfectly calm, but now he began to tremble. It was a responsibility. Liza had wanted the baby, he had not. He would have to live with that. As a scientist, he did not think his conscience was sentimental. Because Yasha was "in the business," as Dr. Weisser had pointedly said—Yasha winced at the allegation of complicity—the doctor had not hesitated to allow Yasha to sit in the adjoining room. He would rather have waited in one of the outer offices, but the operation was too simple for Yasha to have any schoolboy trepidations about it all. After all, Liza was in the hands of an expert, as Yasha himself had assured her. To which she had retorted with a twisted smile: "An expert . . . practicing the oldest profession in the world . . . next to mine."

Between the night that he had willed her to the decision, and this morning when he had roused her out of bed at six so that they could be here by eight, she had barely spoken to him. Because she had once said that if he were to marry her, she would like to practice Judaism—she thought its occult ways mysterious and beautiful—he had brought her symbolic trifles, a *menorah* made in France with small perfumed candles, and a *Mogen David* with a white pearl at its heart. But she had only smiled at him with the weary patience of someone who is temporarily anodyned and does not wish to be disturbed; after all, her case was terminal, she seemed to say.

"Just lie there and I'll be back in a minute," he heard Mrs. Sledge say.

He wanted to step in and comfort Liza, but what would he say? He dreaded that new look of hers, that look of sorrowful resignation coupled with secret knowledge; she reminded him of a lioness he had once seen silently pacing its cage, measuring its strength, as though it were planning at any moment to leap and be free.

There was a long silence. He could hear Liza sigh impatiently, then groan to herself as she shifted her weight on the table. Then he heard a rustle of sheets, the sound of another door opening, and then the sound of approaching feet—Dr. Weisser's.

Yasha suddenly decided that the look in Liza's eyes had not been secret knowledge at all, nor even fear; it had been hate.

He thought he would try to read, but discovered that for the past ten minutes he had actually been holding a magazine in his hands: on the cover was a picture of a baby wearing the incongruous bandolier of the New Year. He could hear Weisser now, instructing the nurse; Yasha imagined Liza's feet in the stirrups, her wrists buckled down into position so that she would not injure herself by striking out at the nurses, at the doctor—at the world. How Liza must loath that manacling of her wrists—exactly as three white boys had held her down once, on an Alabama roadside. There had been nothing she could do to resist then, and there was nothing she could do now. But that savagery had, at least, been the expression of overwhelming lust, a desire for her body; this could only seem to her a meaningless atrocity.

"I feel sick," he heard Liza murmur; and there was the sound of gagging.

It was all right, Yasha thought. They always felt sick . . . nerves. He stood up, the magazine rolled in his hand like a club; he was unaware that the sweat poured down his back.

"No anesthesia now. Maybe a whiff later . . . since he's waiting . . . No use getting her too groggy to walk," added Weisser.

Yasha sat rolling his magazine tighter and tighter, screwing it till the shiny surface shrieked faintly beneath his wet palms. Perfectly normal procedure, he thought. Very simple. Afterwards, they just take up their beds and walk. . . .

"Now we expect you to cooperate, Miss Little," he heard Weisser say, and Yasha easily imagined him moving his right arm from Liza's inner thigh as he spoke; the image created a slight shock. . . . then he began twisting the magazine again till he could feel the sharp deckle-edged pages cutting his palm.

"Sure. . . . Don't *I* know!" gasped Liza fiercely. "Ah sho' will co'perate. Ain' no nigger woman *ever* not co'perate when white boy say 'spraid yo' laigs.' "

"No use being bitter, Miss Little. Just something women go through. Happens all the time."

"Not to *me!*"

"Just move a little forward, will you? Ease down. That's a good girl. Mrs. Sledge? . . . " Weisser's voice rose in interrogative command; Yasha heard the nurse's huge muscled and padded legs move forward, then pause.

"What *you* gonna do?" growled Liza rancorously. "Hold my head down so's he can rape me? You the Madam here?"

He heard Weisser sigh with exasperation; Liza was not cooperating. In fact, she was upsetting him, not a wise idea for a woman about to be cut to the quick.

"We'll try a local first," said Weisser, while Liza went on grumbling.

"That's right. Shut me up!" she hissed between clenched teeth.

There was a long silence while Yasha watched the clock; the second hand moved slowly, a praying-mantis merging with its habitat of hours, passing unseen, like the day he had left the sanatorium years ago.

Then she began to scream. She cursed the doctor, she cursed Yasha, she hurled foul epithets at the moving mountain who tried to invade her flesh with a needle.

Yasha stood sweating and cursing Weisser, silently: Goddam, you butcher, why don't you put her *out?*

"Miss Little. Please stop. You must stop. We can't help you if you thrash about like that."

"You motherfucker," whispered Liza.

"I think she's got it now," said Mrs. Sledge.

"Oh God, help me," moaned Liza, her voice rebounding from the ceiling in a strange empty echo. "Please help me, God."

They always called on God, thought Yasha. It was worse when they didn't, then they called on *him.*

Liza was no longer screaming. "They just want to murder us all," she moaned. "Won't be satisfied till they murder us all. . . . " all the ferocity had been whipped out of her by alternating sieges of pain and drugs, and she began to cry softly, despairingly, in short, exhausted explosions of breath.

" . . . something under her for that bleeding," Weisser was saying while Liza wept. "If she doesn't stop crying, give her another shot."

But as Yasha expected, Liza did not stop. Instead she continued to cry as if she would never cease—crying, not for her pain but for her black mother in Alabama, for the hundreds of bales of cotton she and her mother had picked with bleeding fingertips, pound by pound, in the boiling sun; for the father she had never known, whiter than Yasha, a blonde burning god who had seared through her mother's womb like a fuse: after Liza's birth there had been no more children. Her mother had looked upon her own subsequent barrenness as a curse upon herself for having cohabited with bright and golden Lucifer himself . . . And now, in turn, they had destroyed the white seed of Lucifer's daughter before it had ripened. So Liza wept. She wept for her Janus-headed world, for her hatred and for her love, and for the stigma that Yasha had slashed upon her with a knife. She wept for the passions which had been released upon her, yielding no posterity, but only soiled linen or self-inflicted pain (a knitting needle, her mother used to say would suffice, or a burning blast of castor oil through the belly). But her black mother had never been so efficient as these white men, Kalokovich and Weisser. This time, in cutting out their seed, they had plucked it out by the root, love and all. And Liza hated them all, the white robber barons who had sacrificed her youth and forced her to destroy the fruit thereof—hated them all, including Yasha.

But now Weisser was saying with a great sigh. "O.K. . . . get her up. Give her plenty of codein. Get her on her feet before she starts up again. Slowly. We don't want any vomiting. . . . "

Yasha was standing at the slatted door when the mammoth nurse opened it to allow him to lead Liza home. For a moment Yasha could see nothing: the sheer bulk of Mrs. Sledge filled the doorway. Weisser was removing his rubber gloves, his brows raised significantly: get her out of here, was all Yasha could read in Weisser's face. He wanted to express a word of thanks, or perhaps even an expression of professional sympathy to his colleague (he realized Liza had made the business wretched for Weisser), but his feelings were grotesquely distorted. He found himself furious with Weisser, as if instead of helping him out of a jam he had in fact done him, Yasha, an injury. He could bring himself to say nothing; he merely clenched his teeth as Mama used to do during those last days when she had prepared herself for an eternity of silence.

He moved to Liza's side. She was leaning weakly against the table, supported by Mrs. Sledge. On the sheet not yet stripped away by the all-efficient nurse, lay furls of Liza's darkened blood. Suddenly Yasha could remember a moment, long ago it seemed now, when they had first become lovers and Liza had cut her finger; he remembered how he had taken the injured finger in his lips and with tender cannibalism had promised: "I shall eat you alive. . . . " It seemed to him now that he could again taste Liza's blood, and the thought made him sick.

Mrs. Sledge helped Liza on with her clothes, and within five minutes he and Liza were out in the dimly lighted hallway, trying to find the elevator.

At this point he stopped. When he had arranged Liza's

appointment, he thought he had carefully considered everything —the earliest hour in order to avoid meeting acquaintances in the street, the timed arrangement for a taxi for Liza because he himself would have to hurry back to the hospital, the necessary eight hundred dollars in cash, *not* a check (the bastard, he added as he stood there: he was certain Weisser's usual rate was six hundred). But the one thing that had not occurred to him when he and Liza had entered Weisser's first floor office was that there was no elevator in the building. Now Liza was leaning heavily against him, her eyes half-shut with the concentrated dullness of one ignoring pain. With a glance, Yasha took in their physical situation. The stairs were steep and narrow, with shredding patches of carpet nailed down on each step. From the top of the stairs where they stood, he could see the glint of a brass intaglio laid in the tiled floor below; it gleamed upward, birdlike in shape and fitted into place by bits of white tile projecting from beak, tail and wings. . . .

Slowly he began to guide Liza downward, using the intaglio as a guide. But as they descended, the hallway seemed to become darker, as if the daylight which had made an oblique ray like a pencil mark at the keyhole of the door had been suddenly snuffed out. He tried to rest Liza's hands on the thick wooden banister, but she groaned and slumped down into a corner of the stairway, staring with glazed eyes like a stubborn and sullen drunk. He knew, however, that she was not resisting him but merely coping with her pain; that, animal-like, she did not wish to be disturbed. He would have to carry her. She was light, of course, but was she light enough? The futile, rotting treads of the staircase made it precarious; he himself was not in good physical condition. He began to ease forward, keeping his back against the banister for support; thus, with Liza in his arms he slowly edged his way downward, a step at a time. As they drew nearer, the gleam of brass took on the definite outlines of a bird, but a strange bird, with exquisite tail-plumes like a lyrebird.

In the shabby unpainted squalor of the hallway (a squalor which Weisser used as a disguise to ward off police suspicions of opulence) the brass bird shone with a brightness almost

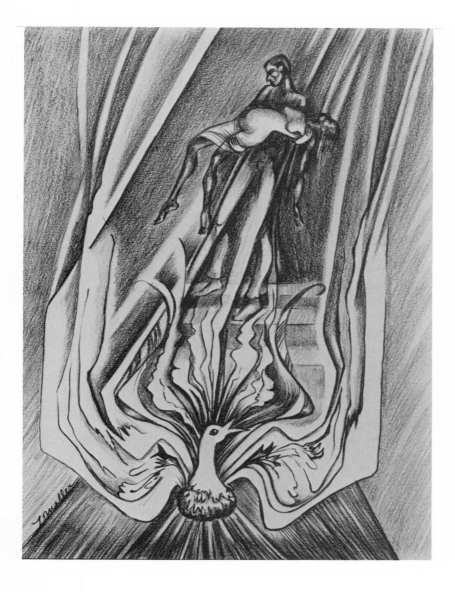

holy. Either this entrance was rarely used or some devoted superintendent lavished an artist's love on this intaglio, which lay, bright and unbruised, at their feet.

He eased Liza to her feet as he opened the heavy outer door. The rarely used hinges gnashed like teeth as they moved out into the deserted street. Clearly he had taken the wrong exit; there must be another entrance where, perhaps, the taxi was waiting . . . With an immense sigh of relief Yasha spotted the taxi cruising about a hundred yards down the street— obviously waiting at another door; when the driver saw them he drove straight towards them. Yasha stood in the chill morning air, his arms tightly around Liza. At last he lifted her into the taxi; she lay with her head sinking awkwardly into a corner of the seat. Hastily he stripped himself of his overcoat and placed it under her head; the gesture made him shrug ironically: the hangman making his victim comfortable.

Liza's eyes opened wide as she became conscious of everything around her; she caught at his hand, sensing his imminent departure.

"You're not coming?" She stated it as though it were a prophesy.

"I've got to report to the hospital first, I'll stop by in an hour or so . . . as soon as I can get away."

She was silent; she relinquished his hand. "Does he know where to go?" she asked, closing her eyes again.

"Cortland Street," he told the driver. "And go slowly. Stay off the car tracks. Better take the freeway."

The driver nodded in a surly way intended, perhaps, to hide his curiosity. Or perhaps he knew, thought Yasha; perhaps every cab driver in Detroit knew this address. Yasha slammed the taxi door shut and watched them drive away. As the cab skidded around the corner Yasha realized that the streets were wet and there was a drizzle of cold rain.

When he arrived at the apartment an hour later, he was alarmed to see that she was bleeding profusely, not in the first pangs of menstrual flow as was to be expected but with a thin bright non-coagulant flow which gushed out on the white sheets. He waited only ten minutes more; then he could stand it no more and called an ambulance. He instructed Liza briefly as to what to say when the internes arrived (he knew they would at once recognize a D & C hemorrhage, and begin asking significant questions). He was not at that moment thinking of his own criminal involvement; he was concerned for Liza's safety. He shot Liza full of antibiotics and Vitamin K and tried to calm himself with the recollection of how her finger had stopped bleeding almost as soon as he had applied his lips to the wound. When he heard the ambulance arrive he went downstairs to give directions.

There was a half-hearted questioning on the part of the hospital staff, but Liza stuck to her story. She refused to tell the name of the doctor who had performed the operation; she had called Dr. Kalokovich, she said (cleverly mispronouncing his name), because she understood that he was willing to come on emergency calls to care for black patients. At this reference to herself as "black," the two staff doctors who had gathered around her bed (in a spirit of friendliness, it seemed to Yasha, rather than in malice) charitably refrained from exchanging glances over Yasha's head. Liza claimed that she was married, but that her husband had deserted her—a common enough story. The doctors nodded professionally. When she had finished her fabrications, she lay back in the white bed of the hospital and folded her hands over her flat stomach; she stared intently awhile at the domelike structure she had created with her pale fingers; then, with a sigh, she closed her eyes and did not even pretend that she was asleep. The doctors, including Yasha, left.

Liza stayed in the hospital two weeks, during which time she refused to see Yasha again. She simply wished to change her doctor, she said. . . Yasha was told later that she had been released into the care of a woman who introduced herself as Sister Nzginga, a woman as black as anthracite, and wearing the long white dress of the Muslims.

After that, whenever he called her, she hung up on him—without a word, without crashing the receiver down on him, but merely returning the phone silently to its cradle, like an

110

oar stilled in darkness. Several months later, when Yasha, in hope of a reconciliation, stopped by her old apartment, he found a star and crescent on the door; but Liza herself had moved away.

Yasha and Moseley sat in a local bar not far from Yasha's office.

"Well, what would you call it: love?" demanded Moseley: they were talking about Liza's abortion.

The use of this word always made Yasha surly. People used it so casually; it was like describing God, the universe, the planets; it was the blind man's description of the elephant.

"Well why not love? Just because I don't want to have any kids doesn't mean I don't love her. A man's got a right to decide for himself whether he wants to make babies. Pointless to let a woman's sentimentality overcome him. Look here, Moseley, I've seen the actuarial records; I'm a doctor. I know what my life chances are. So Liza's twenty and the whole world's rosy to her. But to me it's a polluted mess: too many steel factories, jet planes, coal mines, oil wells, chemical plants, nuclear reactors: and above all, too many people. Now add to this the problem of bringing up a kid who's neither white nor black in a racist society and you've got a potboiler. I should marry Liza, have a dozen kids and write the story of my life: it'd be a best-seller."

Moseley tapped his drink with his finger-nail, thoughtfully: "That's not the way it looks to her. I'll bet it doesn't matter one iota to her that one day we're going to have ten billion people in the world. She wants her happiness just like any person; and she wants it now. If having your baby was what Liza wanted, why what the hell—I just don't see how you've got any kick coming. Whyn't you let her have her baby? I'm sorry," he added quickly as he saw Yasha's scowl.

"You know I'm all for you, Yasha. But I just don't see it . . ."

"It's not just *her* baby, or wouldn't have been, I mean. It'd be *my* kid too. *My* responsibility. If I had a kid I'd want to be sure I was going to be around to teach it things. Like how to stay out of wars and how not to destroy people. And those years in the Sanatorium taught me something I'm not ever going to forget."

"What's that?" Moseley swizzled his drink, a faintly skeptical look in his eye.

Yasha tried to divert himself as well as Moseley from what he felt to be the embarrassing intensity of his reply. Before answering he turned to signal the waitress, then observed with what he thought was enormous coolness: "That people die."

He was glad Moseley refrained from laughing at the platitude; it had certainly been no laughing matter for *him*, barely into his teens and already coping with overkill. . . . His bout with Death had taught him the meaning of time; *tick, tick, tick*: every third thought his end.

Moseley shrugged resignedly. "I just don't see how not letting Liza have this baby helps *you* live."

Yasha looked away, annoyed. It exhausted him to have to argue this way with the people he loved. They didn't know, they couldn't know what it had been for him to lie in a hospital bed day after day, week after week, watching his life, like a giant suppuration, ooze away in thermometers, fever charts, sputum bottles, antibiotics: until, finally, the decision had come to collapse his lung—the pneumo-thorax surgery which had released him, a permanent invalid, from the Sanatorium into the struggle of "normal" men.

He had been able to accustom himself, if without resignation, to it all—to the thermometers and sputum bottles, to the fever charts and x-rays and to the bed rest; he could endure the night sweats, and the toxins, that, like strong drink in his system, kept him alternately exalted and exhausted; he could bear the mild and unimaginative food and the concupiscent and unimaginative nurses (both male and female); he could even endure the lack of anything substantial to read in the Michigan Sanatorium which, after spending $2.56 daily on his physical needs alone, had nothing to spare, consequently, for encyclopedias, scientific journals, philosophers or pessimistic books from an impotent and fallen France.

He had even overcome his very real fear, by reading about the infinite varieties of pulmonary death in books which Moseley brought to him in "shoe" boxes, as though Yasha were a prisoner filing himself out of a ninety-nine year sentence, with the small but sharply perseverant weapon of a library card. He had learned not to notice the flare of his pulse as he read such sanguinary prophecies as: "the average time from infection to death in endogenous progression is thirteen years" or to wince at the necrophilia of a summarizing note in a medical journal: " . . . a better understanding has been greatly facilitated by the study of twelve hundred autopsies at the Municipal Sanatorium."

At first, such unflinching statistics had thrown him into despair: he would die; it was quite clear from these records that he would die—and at the very beginning of his life; he would die without having transcribed a single syllable in this unintelligible tongue of life. Not a mark of distinction would appear on his tombstone. Not "This one died for love or money"; or "Dulce et decorum est pro patria mori," or "Here lies one who believed. . . . " Believed what? He had not yet lived long enough to know what it was he believed. Ah, he wanted to live that he might believe: not *credo ut intelligam*, as St. Augustine had said, but *vivo ut intelligam*. He recalled with shame the bravado with which he had proclaimed to Moseley: "I'd rather die than—" Than what? Than ask his father for money! What nonsense! There was nothing he would not do rather than die—cross burning mountains or floods of ice, march with starving guerillas—rape, plunder, murder—what were stealing and begging compared to this? And if any one had said to him, as he lay on his bed now, "*Die*, or—" with what a howl of liberation would he not run to accomplish the unimaginable "or." It seemed to him that for the first time he could understand all human degradation; man's ultimate debasements, the descent into pimping, miserliness, murder, were attempts to grab more life for the individual—more and more.

Yet so far as his particular life was concerned, the statistics seemed clear. He lay back on his pillows during the first four months when he was on twenty-one hour a day bed rest and read from the books Moseley brought him. In one sanatorium of seventy-eight beds, ninety-seven patients had died over a three-year period. Over a twenty-year period, in treatment using collapsed lung and pneumothorax, more than half the patients were now dead. In Detroit *in this very year* there were 2,468 tuberculars in sanatoria. Of these, ten percent of the white patients and thirty-five percent of the black patients would be dead within three years. At the edict, Yasha's conscience trembled; when he saw his black fellow-prisoners wandering about the halls (the house of Death was integrated), he ticked them off mentally, and he thanked God that he was not black, just as a child in the synagogue he had thanked God that he had not been born a woman. He and Moseley had had a bitter laugh over the strange gratitudes of the white man.

When Yasha had first begun reading the stuff Moseley brought him—Moseley did not know what those books were doing to his temperature—Yasha had gnashed his teeth with rage at these men whom he liked to call his "fellow-physicians," who blazoned forth their ignorance as though it had been a coat of arms. "We do not know," they confessed to each other in their research papers. "We are not sure. There are mysteries. . . . The *cause* of the growing of bacilli are still unexplored frontiers in tuberculosis. . . . " High priests of a profession which held the key—if not to life-everlasting, then to perpetual and recurring Death. Before Yasha was finally "liberated" from the sanatorium, like the countries which like him were under successive waves of attack from the enemy, he was to see the fulfillment of their Statistic, the transformation of his fellow-patients by an invisible process of combustion into dust and bone.

He had taken a dangerous downward lurch in his second year. During the first year the x-ray technician had informed him that several lesions were mysteriously and wholly of their own genius encapsulating themselves, and Yasha had congratulated himself on the mercy of an ignorance which was content to leave well enough alone and let him heal himself . . . But suddenly in his second year there had been "endogenous" reinfection; the right upper part of the lung had been attacked by bacilli "leakage"; and he had found himself in the throes of a combat for his life as real as that threatening the lives of his high school friends fighting in Europe and Africa. The doctors, eventually, had resorted to surgery, and the collapsed lung was slowly healing. During that time he had subsisted on half rations of air except for the 100 c.c. he received at regular intervals; had subsisted on zero rations of love except what he allowed himself in waking or sleeping dreams, choosing his succubus at random from among the nurses; and finally, had subsisted on an intellectual pabulum so lifeless that his very brains seemed to him to have withered and died. It was to this last deprivation, in spite of all the psychiatric social worker could tell him, he found it impossible to "adjust": to the mortal tedium of the unwakened mind.

"Better in hell with a sage than in heaven with a fool," had been one of Mama's favorite proverbs. But one situation which Mama's repertoire had evidently never foreseen was that one might find oneself in Hell—without a single solitary sage. In spite of Yasha's every effort he was bored, bored, bored, by the conversation of the other men in his ward. Their passion was playing cards, and in or out of bed they managed to continue their games—pinochle, gin rummy, poker (open and closed), twenty-one or blackjack, solitaire (in groups), a prehistoric revival of pishe-pashe—and for supreme aimlessness, for an ennui and soporific thicker than ether, they played a game called "Battle" in which, simply and unthinkingly, the higher card won each round over its adversary. With implacable fixity they played this game hour after hour while from their radio came news from the Maginot line, from Roumania, from the Battles of Britain, of Dunkirk, Norway, Denmark, Morocco, the Suez. On the day the Nazis launched their second Russian offensive, which was not to end till the Russians declared Stalingrad safe over a year later, several men in his ward announced that they had played out more sets of "Solitaire" than ever before: they had beat their own record.

Toward Yasha they felt a diffidence vaguely hostile—as if, since he was clearly an "intellectual," he must also be "putting

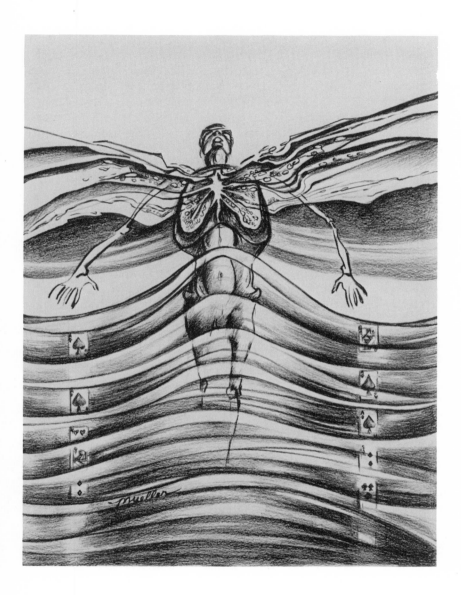

on airs"—else why would he be reading a writer like Andre Gide—obviously one of those "fairy frogs" who hadn't even been able to stand up to the *Boches* like their fathers before them? Once Yasha had gone from bed to bed showing his fellow-patients the Walker Evans' photographs of tenant farmers in overalls. The men in his ward had looked at the pictures and had exchanged significant glances, building around themselves that wall of silent solidarity—hostile, ostracizing—which insulates those who wish not to be disturbed from those for whom the quiet life is for the dead.

There had for a while been several patients in the ward who, humbling themselves before his superior Education ("graduated from high school at fifteen, the guy must be a brain"), had asked him to recommend something to read, to pass the time away. Ignoring pedagogy's first premise, to "start at their level," he had launched into an oral reading of the *Phaedo*, feeling that the problem of the immortality of the soul might have some relevance here . . . But the guys had simply asked him, "personally" and with solemn desperation: "*was* there a physical Resurrection? And if so, what about the basket cases in this war, these paraplegics? . . . "

After that the audience for the *Phaedo* had somehow dwindled away. Yasha had no answers, *personal* or otherwise, to the war: it was the war which was eating at his very insides, leaving "moth-eaten" lesions on his lungs, virulent and suppurating. It was the war keeping him awake, would not let him take his much-needed sleep. While the whole world, by a monstrously accelerated cycle, was being reduced again to its primitive elements of water and stone, he, Yasha Kalokovich squatted in his glassed-in environment, artificially sustained— floating as if alive but, to all knowledgeable circus-onlookers, clearly nothing but a two-headed monster floating in a bottle: and dead.

There was some pyrrhic pleasure in seeing himself that way; his sense of shame was softened by the violent injustice he did to himself. It was the only attenuation he was allowed for the agony of hearing of the never-ceasing deaths of his friends, during those long hours when he lay quietly on his back, seething, healing.

One day the ward physician had informed him he had a visitor. It had turned out to be Solly Levene, a Jewish kid from high school, a boy Yasha had not talked much to but who, it was somehow clear, had always admired Yasha. Solly was a square-toothed unprepossessing kid with plenty of pimples worn like a freshly cleaned oilcloth—the design shiny but the whole surface ravaged . . . spotty and pecked through. Over one eye he had a perpetual shank of hair. The whole structure of his head was like some ill-fitting disguise. As it turned out, the clumsy garments of a clown had concealed the soul of a hero. The guy had come on like a combination Nathan Hale and Theodore Herzl.

Grinning shyly he had placed his new officer's cap on a rack above the night stand. He had obviously made inquiry about the visiting hour and even brought his own lunch, offering to share it with Yasha. As he raised his thin-shouldered, still-boyish body as high as he could to reach the shelf, pushing his cap out of the way of linen towels, washclothes, and paper cups, Solly seemed flushed with the heat of the place: they kept the Sanatorium unnaturally warm. Perspiration had stood on his pale skin, dampening his hair, and under his armpits two dark-brown scars of khaki flowed from the sleeves of his other-wise flawless shirt. Solly mopped his brow as he pulled up a chair beside Yasha's bed. He began slowly, self-consciously, to unwrap a chicken sandwich he had picked up at the drug store. Solly apologized for the hurried visit; he had heard Yasha was sick, had been wanting for some time to visit him. After all, he added self-deprecatingly, although they had never had time to get to know each other, still, they were in this together, weren't they? So he'd come by before shipping out.

Yasha was uncertain what it was they were into together, so he had asked in the warmest tone possible: "Shipping out? Where to?" He tried to remember how old the kid was. It didn't seem possible this pimply kid whose voice was just achieving its first sure masculine resonances could be qualified to lead others into or out of danger.

"Shipping out? Where to?"

Solly's face grew thoughtful; unconsciously he pulled his

shoulders straighter, swallowed a bite of his sandwich.

"Anywhere. *I* should complain. This is our war after all."

"Ours?" Yasha yanked the sheet so hard it fell off the side of the bed; he pulled his knees up toward his chin and sat staring at Solly. He was acutely aware of the contrast between his cotton pajamas and Solly's impeccable uniform.

"Never before have the Jews been so involved in an international situation. What kind of a person wouldn't want to fight a madman who wants to destroy all our people? And after the war our people will have a nation in Palestine—the British won't be able to hold us off any longer."

The reiterative use of "our" annoyed Yasha without his knowing why. "On the contrary," he said with something like surprise at himself—he had not expected to go so far: "I hope there aren't *any* nations—I hope there's just a United States of the World."

"It'll be the greatest thing in the history of the Jews if we can get Palestine away from the English—"

"—and the Arabs—"

"For the first time we'll have a country of our own."

Yasha stirred uneasily beneath the bed covers. "Yeah? What's to stop a bunch of nuts from blowing you off the face of the earth?" Yasha leaned over to one side and yanked a cardboard suitcase from under his bed; it was filled with books. He pulled one out, thumbed quickly through the pages, then handed the book to Solly. "Here, start reading from the middle paragraph where it says"—Yasha read aloud in that hurried monotone meant to indicate to another at what point he should read:

> The cyclotron is the most important single tool to release the enormous pentup energy of the atom. When the cyclotron bombardment becomes sufficiently powerful, this bombardment will itself release vast additional quantities of slow neutrons which in turn will attack more uranium atoms and so on in a chain reaction. . . .

But Solly's gaze flew over Yasha's head, avoiding the book as though it were an immodest woman tempting him away from his chaste study of *Torah*. "Yasha, I'm not too hot on physics, I guess. . . . But one thing I know: this is a real war, not a made-up one. . . . I could be reading philosophy. I could be reading Maimonides, Aristotle. But listen, those Nazi Panzers mean business. The howitzers are making compost-piles of . . . " His reedy voice shook with emotion " . . . of my people . . . . I don't have time to worry about what the Big Brains are planning *after* the war. The war is now. *Here*." He glanced with embarrassment around the Sanatorium ward, then added with a rush, as if he feared Yasha would contradict him and his convictions would fall apart—at least on the rational level: nothing, it was clear could have changed his emotions. "It's not my duty as an officer to study what a cyclotron is . . . My duty as an officer is to take care of my men. To keep my men alive. And myself too," he added apologetically, as though he wished to be pardoned this unpardonable egoism.

Yasha fell silent, ashamed. While he had been frantically raising his hand like an eager schoolboy showing off a bit of knowledge, Solly was quietly putting his life where he felt it counted: to save the world, for Something, for Somebody, Somewhere.

He put out his hand. "I'm sorry, Solly." The weakness engendered by his illness (he thought) brought tears to his eyes: the damned fever permeated everything. "God knows I'd rather not be in this place." His voice broke and he dared not trust himself further. He felt like a coward and a fool, simultaneously. He wanted to cry out, "You're right, you're right," not so much because he shared Solly's vision, but because he yearned to be a man in good health and a "part of all that he had met," and Solly's fate was the fate of his generation. He felt utterly ashamed to be sitting in his bed like a dog on a dunghill while the whole world was facing up to Solly's choice: death or heroism or both.

"Can I get a coke here?" Solly had asked with sudden tact, saving Yasha from what he would later have thought of as rash sentimentality. Solly took some coins out of his pockets, jingled them loudly, as a distraction.

"You can get milk. Buckets of it. Six times a day if you want."

Solly shook his head lugubriously. "Never mind. I'll just have some water. Then I got to rush, I guess. But you think they'd at least let you have some beer or something around here, to . . . to liven up the place." He glanced shyly out of a corner of his eye, fearing he might have insulted Yasha.

"We'd all be alcoholics before the year was out. The boredom and the loneliness are more destructive than the disease: I sometimes think," he added in a more professional tone.

"I guess you weren't meant for the . . . I guess you weren't cut out for *abstinence*."

The modest, awkward word forced a smile to Yasha's lips; but he felt like howling: "No, no. You're damned fucking right I'm not cut out for this monastery!"

"Say, have you heard about Ida Cash?" Solly asked.

Yasha shook his head glumly and glared as a man with an ulcer will glare at spicy dainties on a banquet table.

"She . . . um . . . she got married."

Yasha sat up in surprise. Then they began grinning at each other in mutual recognition of their long-forgotten adolescent yearning for Ida Cash. It was in this mood that Solly had left. With a quick handshake the two men had managed to express their belief that their unexpectedly renewed friendship could never be lost to so stupid an enemy as war. Yet since the war they had seen each other only rarely. . . .

"See you in Palestine," said Yasha as Solly stood on the other side of the elevator cage, his thumb pressed on the button. "Who knows: maybe we'll work in a *kibbutz* together . . .

"Who knows?" echoed Solly, as though it were a response in a ritual prayer. Then he smiled, raising his hand in a sheepish parody of salute: "At ease, Private Kalokovich," he growled, and disappeared in a funnel of air, leaving only two vibrating cords where the cage had stood.

A few days later his sister, Anna, had shown up for one of her irregular visits (she hated to come to the Sanatorium, because it reminded her of Mama's death there). She came dressed in a rose-colored suit which set off her dark hair and hazel eyes. Indeed, he had never seen his sister looking so groomed and pretty and gladly he told her so: she had had little enough flattery of this kind over the years.

"You look as pretty as a picture—like Velasquez' mistress, for example," he said with gorgeous flattery, deliberately over-stating the case so as not to embarrass her with his very real admiration.

"Nobody's mistress," his sister announced, with what he was somehow surprised to realize was a true blush; "but a bride."

"Aha!" he sat up with alacrity, awaiting explanation. "And who's the lucky guy?" But he already knew, with some mis-giving, that it must be Gio Vittore. Although he himself had no objection, of course, to the guy's being Italian, Papa (they both foresaw) would have plenty of objection.

Anna looked at him as if insulted; but her joy came through in spite of her faint frown of protest. Her youthful mouth shaped the name tenderly: "Gio."

"And how do the Vittores feel about it?" he asked in the detached, hearty voice of Anna's neighborhood physician.

"Well, it's not the Vittores, of course. Mr. Vittore was never a practicing . . . never a believer. It's Papa. . . . "

"Well, Papa's not a *believer* either. He's a hater."

"You ought not to be so hard on your father," she said as if possession were nine-tenths of filial affection. "He's so worried about you, Yasha, you can't imagine."

"No, frankly, I can't. A few bucks at the right time and I might never have landed in this hole in the first place. *Now* he's worried, *now* that it's not costing him anything . . . Free room and board for . . . the duration." He turned his head away, swallowing the emotion that seemed to have lodged, palpably, in his throat. "He knew I was working three jobs at once, trying to make it through pre-med. Did he so much as ask if I had enough to eat that time I met him . . . here, here right here. . . . I was on my way to see Mama—" Tears of rage filled his eyes at the recollection.

"Please. You'd better not talk about it. Your fever . . . you know? Better forget about all that and get well. And pardon Papa his . . . well, you know how he is . . . "

*Pardon him*? A gallows pardon him, thought Yasha as he remembered now how he had met his father on his way up to visit Mama in the "C" ward of this very sanatorium. Suddenly he and Papa had found themselves awkwardly juxtaposed in the same elevator—without speaking—Yasha on the way down, Papa on the way up.

Yasha had not wanted to visit his mother again. He was in the habit of making the trip to the outskirts of Detroit at least once a month, and it was exhausting, especially after a morning's work at the radio station followed by late afternoon lab courses at the university. By five o'clock on that day, he remembered, he was thoroughly sick of cutting up frogs and had decided he was certainly not meant to be a surgeon, whatever other kind of doctor he might manage to be. It was Friday. Then in sudden spasm of guilt because he had not been to see Mama all month, he had steeled himself for the ordeal of three street car changes in a fierce fall of snow which always seized him by the throat like a wolf, leaving him choking for air. He refused to admit to himself that not only was he weary and hungry, but also afraid: what he had read of tuberculosis had not reassured him that merely because she refrained from kissing him that his own susceptible lungs were safe. . . .

But the thought of Mama lying on the white metal bed, her hands folded in front of her, staring at the stalk of dying light of her transom window, had urged him on. So pulling down the earflaps of his woolen cap—which would have been out of date even in Kerensky's time—he headed uphill against the wind. Finally, at the entrance to the sanatorium, he turned his back to the wind and stood, panting, choking—but not coughing. Whenever he came to the sanatorium, he heard such a variety of coughing that his own asthmatic gasp seemed a self-pitying indulgence; consequently he had learned by a superb effort of will to convert his gasping into a not-too-telltale breathlessness. Then he went upstairs. Mama's case was more serious this time; she was in Ward C. There were five wards in the sanatorium, and the patients were not at all deceived as to the symbolic significance of altitude. No visitors were allowed in Ward E except the next of kin, or a rabbi. One day when Mama had first been interned, as Yasha had entered the self-service elevator, he had pressed the wrong button and had gone down to what appeared to be the basement, as the ceilings were lined with pipes. He had stood still, waiting for the automatic cycle of sliding cage, receding door and closing crash as the cage-hook reinserted itself, and, as he stood there alone in the narrow boxlike elevator, he heard the frightened wail of a child: "Mum—meee. Help me, Mum-mee." Then a sound like vomiting, the clatter of porcelain receptacles and the whisper of nurses' feet. He had pressed the elevator button with all his strength, as if survival depended on his thumb. He had been so shaken by the experience that he had regretted having come; but at that time Mama had already been in the hospital several months and he had visited her only twice.

Her most recent hospitalization had come as a shock to them. Although she had been ill before, for several years Mama had gone apparently untouched by sickness. In her passion for life—or her ignorance—Mama had, in her brief spell of blooming, given birth to another daughter whom she promptly named after her own mother: Zhenia. That final gift to the Kalokovich family—Zhenia was a bright child with an elfin look of loneliness and of mischief (Mama was too exhausted to take care of her)—that final gift had turned out to be Mama's ultimate sacrifice. Suddenly one sultry afternoon in Papa's store as she was lifting a peck of potatoes to the scales, she had groaned and begun to cough up long streaks of blood. In terror at the sight of her own blood Mama had fainted.

On this particular Friday of a bitter winter afternoon he had found Mama lying in the dark, because it was Shabbos and she would not commit the sin of turning on a light. She was patiently awaiting the nurse—or eternity: whichever came first, with the pious surrender of the Chassidim.

Yasha flicked on all the lights, both in the ceiling and the lamp beside her bed, with a gesture of irritation and, almost, of challenge. And Mama, looking at him gravely, commented:

"What are you, a Shabbos goy that you come in the dark to turn on the lights for the 'fanatical Jew'? —am I not punished enough for my sins?"

"Fanatical is right, Mama," he had said, almost lecturing her. Later, when she was beyond tenderness, he had asked himself, why didn't I kiss her, at least on the cheek? I didn't kiss her at all.

Now he attempted to disguise his dismay at the sight of two bright patches of fever in her face; the flushed cheeks heightened the transparency of her eyes; he felt that if he tried, he could see through them to her soul. She had lost twenty pounds.

"Have you had your supper yet?"

"Ach! Supper, yes. They feed you like a *chazer* here. Ready for slaughtering."

"Perhaps if you had more air? . . . " He looked vaguely around the room, at the windows slanted so they opened like transoms at the top, at the small radio beside Mama's table and at the empty bed on the other side of it.

"Where's your neighbor, Mrs. Zimmerman?" he asked before he had time to reflect.

"Oh!" Mama groaned, not with pain but with a kind of bitterness. She sat up to talk, resting her hands childishly on her knees. "They took her away. 'To another ward,' the morning nurse says. 'Which one?' I asked her. 'I'll send her a little note, how-are-you?' She says 'Up to Ward B. Mrs. Zimmerman is better, but no notes, please, between patients.' Why not, Yasha? It spreads germs or something? So I try the night nurse. I say 'Take me a little message, please, to Mrs. Zimmerman?' 'Who?' she says. Imagine! '*Who?*' she says, and she took that sick woman's temperature every night for two months! . . . 'Mrs. Frances Zimmerman,' I said, 'I'd like to send her a little note of congratulation.' . . .

" 'Congratulation for *what?*' she asked, very annoyed, like I'm being *meshuggah* or something. So I watch how I say it: 'Congratulations for her birthday' . . . . 'Oh,' she says, and she shakes the thermometer like a musician shakes the what-do-you-call it, he leads the orchestra with?"

"A baton."

"Shakes this *baton* and quick she puts it in my mouth so I can't say one word. Then she says, not looking at me but looking down at her watch, she's reading my pulse—and I gave her something to *read* that time. . . . 'Mrs. Zimmerman hemorrhaged during the night. She's been transferred to another ward. She's having a transfusion' . . . Hand me that small bottle," Mama commanded suddenly. "The one with the rubber stopper." With the experienced deliberation which so resembles casual ease Mama coughed into the recess of the bottle. She wiped her mouth fastidiously with a kleenex. "So . . . that's life," she commented ambiguously: whether her own or Mrs. Zimmerman's was meant, Yasha remained uncertain.

"How's Pa?" she asked.

"Fine."

"You help him out week-ends at least? You don't leave it all to him?"

"All what? Papa took in thirteen dollars yesterday, he told me. Working from eight in the morning till ten at night. But he's trying to get a beer license. He says with a beer license things will pick up."

"Still, remember. Seven days a week. He never gets a rest . . . You stay in the store a while, he takes a little nap. . . . " She paused. "He came to see me last month."

Yasha made no comment.

"Well, what do you expect, Yasha, that he should come every night like an insurance agent?"

"He could close the store early . . . get here by seven . . . " Yasha tried not to sit in judgment. "If necessary, Anna could stay in the store. Or Tante Becky. . . . "

"My sister's a sick woman. You can't expect . . . And Anna: I don't want her at night with those *schwartze*."

She looked at him shrewdly. While she reflected, she sipped water from a glass on the surface of which Yasha could discern particles of dust.

"When you were little, once a *schwartze* came and grabbed a slice of orange out of your hand—do you remember?"

"That was Buddy Johnson. His father was an alcoholic. I remember. They finally moved out to California."

"What I'm trying to say is, you *let* him take it: you didn't

126

even try to get it back . . . You came home complaining to me Buddy took your orange, and when Pa said, 'So why did you let him?' you said, 'I don't know . . . He's my friend,' and Pa said: 'What kind of a friend is that—a *schwartze* who steals oranges?' . . . And you started to cry."

"Well? So what's the point?"

"The point? The point is Papa maybe thinks you'll give away all his oranges, so how can he leave you in the store?"

"Here, give me that damn glass, I'll get you some fresh water." He took the aluminum pitcher and glass out to the night nurse's desk in the hallway and asked drily:

"Where can I get my mother some water?" Upon which she replied that she was coming by in a minute to check Mrs. Kalokovich for the night.

When he returned to the room she was out of bed, wearing a maroon flannel bathrobe faded to the color of old blood. He recognized it as having belonged to somebody, he could not remember to whom; it was catastrophically too large for her. She sat down in an armchair facing the window; Yasha drew another chair for himself.

"Doing all right in school?" She asked in the simple telegraphic way his mother assumed when she knew the answers to her questions.

"What else? Your children always do well in *school,* Mama. It's the *world* that's too much for them."

She sighed: "The world's a lot for anybody . . . Time passes in a flood. Before I knew it, my son was out of rompers into a doctor's white jacket."

"I'm a long way from being a doctor, Mama."

"My sister came to see me," she came to the point abruptly. "A diabetic she is. They stick a needle into her before she can take a bite in her mouth. Nothing else they can do . . . *nu.*" It was a statement and a question.

"Someday, it'll be easier. They're working on insulin."

"Someday . . . Someday . . . My sister is forty-five years old. Me, they're giving something new already. Sulfa-something, I don't know how they say. Only now I have to pass water every hour. Something's with the kidney."

She thought, evidently, that he would know why. "Mama," he said with something like agony. "All I do yet is cut up frogs. Someday—"

"Someday. Someday," she repeated like a litany. "Someday the Messiah will come. Who will be here to see the day?"

Suddenly she rose to part the curtains; the omnivorous bathrobe shrouding her fell away so that he saw with shock the shrunken breasts flattened ruthlessly by the coarse white smock tied viselike at the throat, a smock intended neither for male nor female, mother nor child, but for the ailing poor, bereft of all vanities.

Her hand was not strong enough to pull the heavy cord of the drapes, so she turned away, looking at him with dumb despair.

"I'll get it, Mama. . . . . It's stuck up there at the top." He whipped the cord as if to loosen some unidentifiable knot in the curtain rod; and at that point the nurse entered with the water, a thermometer and fresh sputum bottle, all assembled on a tray. She set the latter on a bedstand.

"She comes every night the same time," Mama announced gloomily. With graceless accommodation she opened her mouth as the nurse inserted the thermometer. She clamped her upper lip over the fragile glass as if determined to remain silent forever.

The nurse studied the record; her routine absolved her from the necessity of sham amenities and she did not speak to Yasha.

After a while Mama herself took the thermometer from her mouth and handed it to the nurse. She was too accustomed to it all to make any show of friendliness for Yasha's sake: clearly the night nurse was not her favorite.

"Nu, how much is it?" she asked, as she would have asked of someone weighing a fish.

"100.4—not bad."

"Same as last night," commented Mama laconically.

"Is it?" The nurse shaped her voice into polite, if toneless, query.

Mama did not speak to her again. When she had gone Mama said:

"Every night she took Frances' temperature, you know Frances—Mrs. Zimmerman. Now, does she speak to me one word about her? Does she answer me a question? *Kalte neshomah!*" To say of a woman that she had a 'cold soul' was Mama's ultimate indictment.

"She's just doing her work, Mama—it doesn't mean she has a cold soul—if she has a soul at all," he added involuntarily.

"*If.*" Mama covered her eyes with her hand, shutting out the world of perishable possibility, looking inward to certainty. "God help him—" she addressed an unseen presence, "he believes nothing; nothing at all. How does it come to me to have an atheist in the house? In Germany the Jews are leaving everything behind, running, running to England, America, Argentina, so they can still wear a tallis and be a Jew. Here, my own son thinks we're made of glass. You think I'll die, I'll break in pieces and nobody will be able to put me back together?"

"I don't think you'll break to pieces. And let's not talk about dying. You've been in this place before, Mama. Sometimes I think Papa's right," he pretended to scold her, "—you *let* yourself get run down."

She was silent. Usually she would react to Papa's mindless thrusts with indignation. This time she sat huddled in the huge clotted bathrobe as if she were cold.

"Never in C. Always I was at the top. Never more than six months. . . . "

"Mama—"

"How's Anna," she stopped him—and herself—with determination. "She still goes with that *shagutz?*"

"Gio? I guess. I never see her except going to or from classes. But she's doing a lot of painting now, water colors, oils. . . . "

"Papa knows about the *shagutz?*"

Yasha shrugged. "How do I know what Papa knows? I never see him. . . . You know, since that night, the night of the race riot. . . . "

"He needs you. You need him. You're his son."

"I'm his son—but he doesn't need me. What he needs is a beer license."

"Don't mock your father, Yasha." Then thoughtfully: "You think Anna has talent? It's a crazy thing for a Jewish girl—we never had painters in our family."

"Who knows what talent is? You start out with talent—after that, it's will-power: unless you're a genius."

"But Anna's not a genius?"

"No." He saw that she would have believed him if he had said "yes."

"Then what good is it? It'll make her miserable, that's all. She'll be better off if she takes a nice boy like the baker's boy: what is his name? Irwin-Isadore. . . . Itzik . . . something like that. A hard-working boy, serious. His father was from my *shtetl*."

"There are no *shtetls* in America, Mama."

"There are shtetls everywhere," she asserted. "You go to New York, you'll see shtetls from every country. Here in Detroit, you have the *Polacken*—a shtetl; the *schwartze*, also a shtetl, the hill billies—they don't mix one with the other. They're still like the place they came from."

He refused to be an emissary on this question. "If Anna wants to 'mix' no one can stop her. Least of all, me."

"But he's a *Catholische*. What will she do, go to Mass on Sunday and sprinkle herself with water, she should be holy?"

But again he dissociated himself from this attack, which he knew was directed at Anna.

"You have things to do here?" he asked. "To pass the time? . . . Would you like me to bring you something—some bagel, some halvah maybe? So you can nibble when you get hungry."

"I'm never hungry. . . . So you're going already," she added intuitively. "*Nu*, be careful. It's slippery outside. First it was snowing, then was raining, now the snow's very wet. Dangerous."

"Don't worry about me. . . . " He tried not to emphasize the pronoun. "Take care of yourself."

"For me there's nothing they can do."

"What you need is a new bathrobe," he declared, his voice between a question and a command. Unconsciously his speech had fallen into the Yiddish intonation which made her at ease with her children. He knew she was sadly aware that there were times when she could understand nothing of what her children were saying to each other—especially when they used a richly colloquial American idiom; it was this loss of communication which had grieved her more than any other loss.

"You need a new bathrobe," he repeated almost angrily, surprised at his own fierceness. "That bathrobe makes you look like a skeleton. Who gave it to you anyway?"

She looked at him sharply before she answered. "Nobody gave it to me. Frances Zimmerman, she left it. Do you think they'll come ask for it, she needs it?"

Then, on the way down, by a curious coincidence he had met Papa who was about to get off on the "C" Ward. A moment's hesitation, an awkward pushing of the button and they had found themselves briefly alone together on a bizarre, Kafkaesque ride downward. . . . All the way down to the main floor Papa had stared at the ground, as if he had been momentarily imprisoned with an Evil Spirit, and in order to exorcise it, he must stare at the ground and spit three times. Although Papa had not actually spit, Yasha had felt as annihilated in body and spirit as though he had. When the elevator stopped, Yasha stepped out without a word, without looking behind him. It was the only time he had seen his father since the night of the riots. . . .

Two months later Mama had hemorrhaged badly and Yasha had been summoned from a lab class to the hospital, where he had been obliged to wait two hours in the waiting room before they would let him see her: were they dressing her up for his visit? He had arrived with a headache; holding his head with despair, he had realized that he was running a fever. He observed the fact with a keen sense of indifference, of clinical foreknowledge: the patient's head was burning with fever; the head was his; therefore the fever was his also. He had asked the woman at the switchboard for two aspirin; then for two more: his head was splitting. Reluctantly, she had shaken out a single five-grain tablet. Was he ill, she asked, though without solicitude. To her, people on the "outside" were not ill.

"No, no. Just a headache," he had sense enough to reply. Above all he had not wanted to be sick *in this place*. He had tried not to look exhausted as he staggered back to his chair to wait for them to allow him upstairs. Somewhere between 102° and 103° he said to himself, and afterwards could remember only Mama's eyes.

Evidently he had sat by her bed for hours before she died, and she had not spoken. He could remember only Mama's eyes. His own fever seemed to radiate from her burning eyes; the rest of her face was a white swathe, sunken into a shockingly emptied skull. Lips, once sensuous and full, were sunken; temples and cheekbones projected like some caricature done by a virulent Artist, if not an insane One. She lay covered, except for her face. Her eyes spoke love, love living, love perennial, but her breath spoke only of death. The burning light in those eyes flamed finally to love irrepressible; a single, fractured sound which must have been his name, then something like tears gushed from her eyes to his, and he stood there sobbing over the released body; and then suddenly there was blood everywhere.

At the funeral he had not mourned. He stood to one side of the gathered relatives as though he himself were some sort of suicide, not to be allocated earth-room among these regenerate souls who would die, respectably, in their beds. He was oddly surprised that there were so many of them, relatives of Mama's from New York, Chicago, even California. There was sobbing and hysteria. His sisters wept uncontrollably. Anna was at last led away from the yawning grave, into which they had thrown dirt like rice after a bride. Only there was no bridegroom. Mama had lived alone, standing beside Papa like a tenuous archangel. During her years in America she had never gone farther west than Chicago, had never been to night school or gone on a vacation or driven a car or visited her relatives in New York City. She had arrived in the United States when her new country was at the height of prosperity and prohibition, and she had never tasted alcohol nor cut her long hair, nor worn a short skirt nor owned a raccoon coat. Above all, she had not lived to see *nachos*, good-fortune for her children, which

132

was the prayer of every Jewish parent; she had simply loosened her hold on them in mid-stream and drowned. And in a blindly prejudiced way which he could neither explain nor overcome, Yasha had always held Papa responsible for her early death: older and more cunning than she, Papa had laid upon her the burdens of the store, the children and the flesh with the ruthlessness of one who means to survive himself, at all cost. Pardon *him?*

"You have to learn to pardon Papa," Anna repeated, "just as you would pardon any other mistaken person. Why should you be harder on your own father than on the rest of the world?"

"Why? Because he's my father, that's why. Precisely."

Anna shook her head uncertainly. "It doesn't seem fair. I hope one day my kids . . . your kids . . . "

He interrupted her with sudden irascibility: "Look Anna, you're hardly even married yet and you're already talking about a family. For Chrissake, how do you even know things will work out? Before you tie yourself down with a couple of kids, be sure you—" He stopped, fearful he had offended her.

Anna stared around as if the explanation for it all lay in the row upon row of sick men lying in bed nursing their angers, their griefs, their mortality.

"The food here. Is it good? I mean, is your appetite picking up?"

He shrugged.

"Do the doctors say . . . how long? . . . " Anna ventured.

"Never!" Yasha leaned against the metal headrest of his bed in a semi-reclining position; he fought the sheets with his feet a moment as though they were a flag of the enemy whom he was determined to bring down with his own blood if necessary. Then managing to bring his emotion under control he said: "If there's one thing the doctors are sure of is that they're never sure. They always start with six months here. In my case, after four weeks' *complete* bed rest—that means lying as if you're nearly paralyzed—they estimated a year. At the beginning of the second year, with sputum negative and with a daily fever of around 99°, they said (also) a year—"

He saw his sister's eyes grow wet and he tried to repress an exasperating surge of self-pity.

"But they have drugs now—surgery, that sort of thing. I heard there's something new, they're using it on the wounded. . . . "

"Well, they have sulfathiazole. They sprinkle it around like salt to flavor your ribs and pleura." But he did not want to talk about his illness. "Well, Papa will have to learn how to cook now that you're leaving him. How will he manage without you taking care of him, literally keeping him alive," he added jealously. It suddenly seemed to him his father had rescued his own life from the debris of his, Yasha's, like a looter in a disaster area.

"Oh, he'll get along," Anna said modestly. "He eats like a bird anyway. Like you. . . . " she added with a certain stubbornness, as if Yasha might resent the comparison. "He's had the same breakfast every morning as long as I can remember. Such an unchangeable man in his habits," she murmured. "He spends his whole life in that store . . . " There was no response from Yasha, so she hurried on: "He has no friends or anything; he never goes anywhere. What does he get out of life?"

"Money," asserted Yasha promptly.

She ignored this thrust as predictable and went on with what was clearly becoming a mission: "He asks about you all the time, Yasha. Whenever I come home after visiting you, he says, 'Nu, and the fever?' and I say, 'About the same, but Yasha looks better. . . . ' And he grunts in that way he has, you know and says, 'Maybe they'll let him come home soon, eh?' *Home.* That's what he says. He wants you to come home. So how can you always accuse him of thinking only about his money? He *wants* you to come back," she repeated stubbornly.

After a pause Yasha admitted: "That's what the social worker told me—that he wants me to come home. When I get out."

"Social worker? Hospital sponsored?"

Yasha smiled wanly. "Nothing is too good for the charity patients in the State of Michigan. I think the woman is a plain-clothes psychiatrist. She comes here once a week to try to 're-habilitate' me for the outside world. Anyway she says Papa is a 'very unusual person, quite charming'—as you know he *can* be . . . to strangers."

Anna frowned. "No use being so hostile. Whether you want to believe it or not, these people are very well-trained—"

"Well, damned if I need someone to tell me that what I'm afraid of is dying, and that what I need when I get out of here—*if* I ever get out of here—is money!"

"Do you think—now don't you get angry, Yasha—but do you really think you ought to go on to med school? After all, see what you've done to your health."

"Thanks."

"I didn't mean it that way. I mean, maybe we ought to come to terms with our—limitations."

He glared. "And what terms would you recommend? That I become a veterinarian?"

Tears filled Anna's eyes. "Let's not talk about it then. Since you feel so strongly . . . I only came . . . I only came to tell you the good news. God knows when I'll get a chance to come back here again. We're going to New York for our honeymoon, and who knows: we may stay there . . . And now we're quarreling. All I meant was that a doctor's life is very strenuous —*you* know that."

Instinctively Yasha drew the covers around his body as if to protect himself. To change the subject he asked seriously: "How's your painting coming along? You might have brought a couple of pictures to show me, you know I always liked seeing your work around. You could even hang one up there beside the sputum cabinet," he added gaily.

"I haven't done much painting lately," Anna confessed looking at her hands which were clean and remote.

"Too many bridal showers," he said, trying to make it blithe and joyous; but his disappointment showed through. Since it was no use trying to deceive his sister (she knew him too well), he added with an intensity he thought he had managed to restrain all during her visit: "Don't give up your work, Anna. Don't let any one or anything stop you. Not just to marry and raise kids. After all you've been through to learn how to paint . . . Night schools and Saturdays and painting on the rooftops on hot summer nights . . . Ah, I remember it all . . . " he added admonishingly.

She flushed, whether with pleasure or embarrassment he was not certain. She looked down at the patternless concrete floor, barely covered here and there with daubs of dun-colored tiles. When she looked up again at Yasha there was something alien, hostile in her face which he had never seen before; and in her voice was a thread of ferocity like an untuned violin string—thin and irascible.

"*No one* will stop me," she said.

When his sister was ready to leave he had not walked with her to the elevator; he could not bring himself to wish her joy in her marriage. In the abrupt silence which descended on them both he felt only that he was witness to a long fierce struggle between Anna and Gio which had already begun.

Within the same month Moseley had visited him. Visitors were so rare at the hospital, which took in mainly patients whose families could not afford to send them elsewhere and who naturally had little time or energy to visit, that Yasha began to be a subject of envy among his fellow-patients. First Solly, then his sister and on this day still *another* visitor, the orderly had informed Yasha with a patronizing smile: a Lieutenant Williams was down in the receiving room and wanted to see Mr. Kalokovich, would that be all right? The heavy irony in the orderly's voice made the mingling of names sound like a black minstrel show. . . .

Nevertheless, Yasha was relieved to have even five minutes' advance warning; he rushed to get out of his pajamas and bathrobe, and even considered shaving—as though Moseley were some celebrity whom he wanted to impress . . . He put on a clean suit and was decently dressed when Moseley arrived; when he saw Moseley he was glad he had taken the trouble.

To his amazement Moseley came in the immaculately starched uniform of the Army Air Force, his officer's vizor slanted like a permanent shadow across his tea-colored face. Behind the orbed lens of his eyes, capped with light, his face flashed excitement—quick, restrained, minnowlike. It was a bit of a surprise to him that Moseley was old enough to be an officer; but Moseley had always been shy about personal data; he rarely offered explicit details: about his age, about his childhood in Birmingham, about the mother and sister he had left behind in Alabama.

"So you made it," Yasha announced at once, striving to overcome his jealousy with an honest blend of admiration and bitterness.

Moseley smiled. "You sound as if you don't believe it. Listen, when Uncle Sam needs you to fight, he doesn't ask whether you're black."

"But an officer? . . . " Yasha murmured uncertainly, scarcely knowing himself what he meant. It was clear to him that Moseley was ecstatic over his commission and was controlling his sense of triumph only out of deference to Yasha's illness.

"And why not? I can kill people better and faster than anybody. I've got twenty-twenty eyesight. That means I can see a village or a German munitions factory from my bomber without the least difficulty. And God knows I ain't *color* blind. Sho' don't want no color blind people in the Air Force."

In spite of himself Yasha laughed.

"Well, at least you'll see Europe—"

"Yeah, but I got to blow it all *up* first. . . . "

"You're pretty sure you're going to the European 'theater,' as they call it. . . . "

"Well, I'm *not* sure. Of course they never tell you. Everything you learn is by the grapevine. But it seems right now more likely than the Pacific. Anyway, I hope they *won't* send me to the Pacific. . . . "

"Why?"

Moseley removed his officer's cap thoughtfully and kneaded the scar which the rim had made on his forehead; the mark remained however. "I don't know . . . I just don't want to go playing *hari-kari* with the . . . Japanese people."

Yasha was puzzled. The war was then being fought fiercely in the West—the Nazis were striking toward the Caucasus; Rommel was in Egypt and Libya; the entire Don River Bend was in danger of falling into Nazi hands; whereas in the Pacific they were just beginning to hear of Doolittle's thrusts at Tokyo, and MacArthur's Battles in the Coral Sea and Midway. To those who were not yet totally involved in the titanic struggle, the Pacific was apt to seem remote and sporadic compared to the millions of people struggling outside of Rostov, Stalingrad, and in the Caucasus Mountains. Yasha somehow could not accept the simplicity of Moseley's reply.

"I just don't want any part of Japan, that's all," Moseley repeated, and tightened his heart-shaped mouth.

For a second Yasha wondered whether Moseley's feelings about the Japanese had anything to do with his concept of "white imperialism"; but Yasha dismissed the idea at once as ludicrous. It was only in retrospect that the phrase "Japanese people" was to strike Yasha as odd; for Americans during the war never spoke of them as anything but "Japs." At the moment he had begun instead to talk to Moseley in terms of his personal "invasion" of Europe.

"When you get a look at all those beautiful women over there, you won't want to come home," he said, trying to lift himself out of a growing depression.

But Moseley only smiled sadly.

"Yeah, I hear they don't have anything against black people over there. But I don't want to stay over there. I never have wanted to go there to *stay*. I've got the biggest job in the world to do right here. We've got fourteen million blacks here in the United States—and that's a nation. I'm going to come back here and make my people a *nation*. . . . "

Yasha felt suddenly weary. He shook his head almost indifferently.

"Have you ever heard of CORE?"

"No." Yasha began almost absent-mindedly to rub a spot on his chin which he had nicked while hurriedly shaving. He felt hot and perspiring and he was certain his temperature was rising. But he added politely to show he was listening:

"Core what?"

138

"CORE. Congress of Racial Equality. I'm going to join their movement."

Yasha looked dazed. "What do you mean, you're going to 'join their movement?' I thought you'd just joined the Air Force."

"I mean when I get back. First thing I'm going to do is go out to Chicago and work with the people there. I've already been there—to see what they're up to. . . . And it's a great organization. They got new ideas, ideas that are going to change the world. Only first I got a little business in Europe to polish off. . . . "

"The world?" Yasha cocked his head to one side with ironic disbelief. "It's going to take more than one organization to change *this* world."

"They . . . opt for non-violence," added Moseley, almost irrelevantly.

Yasha sat up in bed; he had irritated the spot on his chin till he drew fresh blood; he tore a piece of paper from a roll on his nightstand and dabbed at the wound. "Moseley, I can't understand you," he confessed. "You're like somebody going two ways at once. You talk about bombing the enemy and about coming home to save the world with non-violence—both at once. At least Gandhi doesn't go off and bomb all hell out of the British, then come back to the Ganges and preach programmed pacifism. . . . " He saw that Moseley was irritated, so he tried to divert their argument by the only sociability allowed at the hospital. "How about going into the recreation room and I'll slip you a little wine. Just some home-made stuff Anna left me."

"Sounds good to me."

He picked up a sterile paper cup for Moseley, then led him down the corridor to the recreation hall; he could not help noticing that compared to Moseley he positively shambled: his weight was down to 130 and he must have looked like a giraffe, with his spindly legs.

As they walked into the recreation room Yasha looked around and tried to see the place, objectively, from Moseley's view. It was a Sunday and the room appeared to its best advantage. The floor had been washed and waxed and it now shone in the sunlight. The windows overlooking the balustrade—not wide enough to be a balcony where the patients might have put chairs outdoors—had been cleaned, and the draperies seemed to move with their own color in the morning light. A few occasional chairs of bright-colored plastic had been scattered around the polished floor; they might have been preparing for a ball.

Most of the patients were at Sunday Church service; thus the hall was relatively empty—a thing rare in itself. But soon the aimlessness of a Sunday afternoon would set in; there would be hours and hours to "kill" before the unneeded lights would dim as if it were truly night, and they would be sent to bed like hapless boys while the corn-colored light was still in the west. Then they would lie awake with their vague fears till sleep overcame them at last, and the sweat of their bodies in fever soaked the sheets. . . .

"I see they got a piano here," Moseley commented as he sat down.

"Nobody ever plays the thing. Except at Christmas. Or when they've had a little to drink. Mostly they just use this room to play cards and write letters."

But it was obvious Moseley was not thinking about the piano. He sat with his knees crossed, his cap balanced precariously over one knee. He pushed the cap around his forefinger so that it spun slowly, like a toy. Then he continued as if he had been silently mulling over Yasha's question about non-violence ever since they had left the ward.

"Yasha, listen to me—what do you expect me to be? A conscientious objector?—a *black* conscientious objector? Who ever heard of such a thing? They'd send me to one of those prisons back home where they'd shoot me like a dog one dark night, or have some other prisoner knife me in a 'fight' and then *parole* the guy that did it. No. Listen. I've got a job to do and I'm going to do it. I don't want anybody saying to me after the war 'What did *you* do? What right have *you* got to be a member of the Congress of Racial Equality? If this is your country, why didn't *you* fight for it?' See? There's going to be a time when questions come up, and I'm going to throw my paratroop boots right in The Man's face, and I'm going to say: 'Look man, while you were here screwing my mother and sister down South, I was falling through three thousand feet of space—waiting for Fascists like you to blow up my silk any second with a bazooka.' So I'm going to fight in this war. This is my kind of war—a war against racism. *You* ought to know that."

Yasha flushed. He tried to assume a calm he did not feel: he felt suddenly the bathos of his pretending to be involved in a future which he might never live to see.

Shortly afterwards, Moseley rose and handed Yasha a package, wrapped in green and gold Christmas paper.

"What's that?" demanded Yasha ungraciously.

"It's a little going away present."

"What for? I'm not going anywhere."

"Well, call it a Christmas present." Moseley was patient, amiable, treating him like the sick man that he was.

"Well, if it's a Christmas present," Yasha said reluctantly, "you're way ahead of your time."

"Not likely I'll be around here at Christmas. And I wanted to give you . . . to leave you something. But I got to run now. Got to be back at the base by morning . . . " Moseley did not hurry, however. He lingered as if he still had much to say. He stood as if in a trance, setting and resetting his cap on his head. There was a faint tremor in his hand as he lit a cigarette; the tiny flare illuminated the wedgelike scar across his forehead over which the cap rested uneasily. He stood another long moment in silence. Yasha held his breath: they were all going—all; and he was left behind like a fly speck on the wall.

"Well, Yasha," said Lieutenant Williams as he laid his brown hand for a second on Yasha's shoulder. "Like they say in the movies: 'This is it.' Don't forget to drop me a line." He pointed briefly to the APO address on the wrapped package, and turned away. As he passed the beds of the other patients there were whistles and catcalls: "Hey Cap'n Jigaboo, where you going with that outfit?" and "What's *that*" followed by a whistle. Without turning to reply, Lieutenant Williams had walked into the corridor.

*But how could he explain all that to Moseley or Liza or his sister without sounding like a lunatic?*

"Well, it just don't make sense to me, Yasha. You tryin to make one big hell of a philosophy out of it and seems to me it's plain as *black and white.* You just too chicken to have a black kid. And I don't blame you! . . . It's enough to scare hell out of you, being black in this here Amerika. (He indicated the new spelling with his index finger.) I mean Ameri-KKKa," he added, coughing the letters like an expectorant. "Look, there's a problem with kids that's bigger than the race problem and that is, are you, Yasha K., going to love it or hate it? . . . "

"Jesus, what a thing to say, Moseley. You wouldn't think of saying that to a so-called *liberal,* now would you? But you think I can take anything from you. Listen, I'm sick of you always plumbing my subconscious, like my psyche were into two layers, black and white. I wish you'd get off my back. Isn't it enough I feel like hell cause Liza hates me without you making problems that don't exist and talking crap about how if I had a black kid, maybe I wouldn't even *love* him? Boy, that's pretty sick. . . . "

Moseley shrugged. "Well, may be I overstated it. But I'm always suspicious when somebody gives me some sociologico-pseudodoxia to help explain anything as simple as love."

"*Simple?* Love? I don't find it so goddam simple. I think Liza hates me. . . "

"Oh come off it. People don't turn love on and off just like that."

"Well, she's been going to see this guy Ibn X or whatever he calls himself."

"She really believe that Muslim stuff—about you white men being the Devil?"

Yasha held his head in his hands. "I don't know. She goes to services regularly. I think she really *wants* to believe it, like my sister was going to Mass with her new husband, till she gave up religion for the Revolution. Actually, I'd like to hear what they've got to say. I'd like to know what I'm fighting: is it for real? They have services every Wednesday and Friday

night. I may just tune in to see what they got to say . . . Come
with me?" He really wanted Moseley to come along, so he
expressed it as a challenge: "Are you game to go?"

Moseley laughed, "No thanks. They can't teach *me* anything
I don't know about the white man . . . Only thing is, they're
going about it the wrong way—you can't hate em, you got
to *love* em. You got to love the Devil if you know what I
mean. You're just hoping to see Liza," Moseley added after a
pause. "Can't say as I blame you. But it might be the wrong
place."

"Look, if I wanted to see Liza I'd go to her and speak to
her, that's all. What I want to do is hear what I'm up against
in this Muslim thing. It's not bad enough Liza and I have to
fight the whole Judeo-Christian tradition, now she's got me in
bad with Allah too. . . . "

He forced himself, finally, to admit: "Come with me,
Moseley. Fact is, I hate being the only white man at the
party. . . . "

"Some switch . . . " observed Moseley dryly. "O. K. then.
What time you say services start?"

"Eight o'clock."

"Well, first I got to go back to the hotel. Shower and all
that. Have to catch a plane for Seattle. But suppose I meet
you there? Outside."

When Yasha and Moseley arrived at the store front temple
on Frederick Street the street lamps were already lit. At the
entrance to the temple stood the guard—a huge, nut-brown Negro
built like a boxer; he wore a black suit with a span of boiled
white shirt and a bow tie. To his coat-collar was attached an
emblem designating him as the Fruit of Islam.

"Peace, brother," he said. "*As-Salaikum.*"

"Wa-Salaikum," replied Moseley at once, touching his own
black face as if involuntarily, then pointing to Yasha: "He's
O. K.," he added.

It was already slightly past eight, and the service was about
to begin. As they walked rather self-consciously toward the
only empty seats—which were, unfortunately, in the front row

—Yasha tried to take in the whole scene; he could not resist turning around in eager curiosity to stare at the congregation. It seemed to him he had never seen black people so passionately calm. There was no chatter, no display of church-going finery. Their simplicity was as urgent and graceful as a panther. The men were dressed entirely in black with white shirts; the women wore scarves covering their hair, and long dresses somewhat like cotton *sari*, giving an effect of exquisite modesty. In the evening quiet they sat charged with light and shadow, motionless—a revolution *in fresco*. What struck Yasha most vividly were the children; they sat beside their mothers with the self-conscious dignity of black princelings: washed and polished to a high gleam as though they were the bright heirs of a future empire.

Not far to the left of where he and Moseley were sitting Yasha had noticed Liza at once; but she gave no sign of having seen him. She stared instead at a blackboard in front of the congregation, on which was written: Who Will Survive Armageddon: the Cross or the Crescent?

Yasha turned to read the messages on the other blackboards. On one had been sketched both the cross and the crescent: under the cross was an actual photograph of a partially decomposed black body, hanging from a tree. Beneath the date of the atrocity someone had written in Arabic-looking script: "The murderers are still at large. . . . " Under the crescent were the words: "Islam: Brotherhood of the Black and Yellow Races." Alongside it was an enlarged photograph of several Chinese doctors at the Kwangtzu Hospital in Shanghai engaged in suturing the blood vessels of rabbits' ears—vessels smaller than human's—in the hope of one day (the photograph explained) being able to reattach severed human limbs. Yasha became so absorbed that he forgot his conspicuous position at the front of the congregation; he leaned forward, straining his eyes to read the caption beneath the photograph. . . . Similar experiments, he read, were being conducted at the Shanghai Municipal Research Institute of Traumatology. Yasha was already copying out the address when he realized that he was becoming an object of attention; he put his notebook away.

A light-skinned Negro walked up to the lectern; at first Yasha assumed that he was their regular minister; but he introduced himself as Brother Sundiata X. He was proud and happy, he said, to see so many familiar faces—and some unfamiliar ones. (It seemed to Yasha that at this point the gaze of the entire congregation converged at the back of his neck.) They had been trying for many weeks, as they all knew, to get Minister Marcus X from Chicago to come here to speak to them. Minister Marcus X, as they all knew, was one of the most dedicated disciples of the Messenger, Elijah Muhammed. Ever since Minister Marcus X had been released from prison seven years ago, he had been making a name for himself and for the Muslims by preaching the faith everywhere in the United States. And now, just this last month, Detroit's very own Minister Ibn X (at this point there was a whisper of approbation) Detroit's very own Minister Ibn X, the light-skinned Negro repeated impressively, had visited the Messenger, Mr. Elijah Muhammed, at his home in Chicago, and while he was there, Brother Ibn X had persuaded Minister Marcus X to come here and speak to them *today*; and now here he was: Brother Minister Marcus X. With a grand flourish the light-skinned Negro, who had apparently been chosen from among the more distinguished members of the congregation to introduce the guest, opened his arms toward Minister Marcus X who had been sitting directly behind the lectern—concealing himself behind the lectern, Yasha would almost have said. A tall, reddish Negro now approached the lectern. Though he gazed down upon the audience he seemed for the first few moments scarcely aware of them. He simply stood quietly, like a slowly heating stone in the desert, listening to the silence which he had created. When his voice rang out suddenly— "Brothers and sisters, sacred and beautiful are all of you in my eyes!"—it was as if the sharp blade of his lip had struck the stone and from out of the desert of silence, words flowed. The congregation stared at him and drank.

There were another few seconds of silence, not of hesitation, but of fury; then Minister Marcus X thrust his tinted glasses fiercely to his nose; the tiny metal nosepiece bit harshly into the soft skin, spanning the bridge of nose with the flared nostrils which dilated as he spoke. Scars of sleeplessness ringed his eyes, but his voice showed no fatigue. From his pocket Minister Marcus X took out a white notebook which he seemed about to place in the center of the lectern; then Yasha caught a glimpse of a strong aztec-colored hand, as slowly Marcus X picked up the notebook, gripping it between thumb and forefinger, like some floating fragment caught between the limbs of a colossus. He riffled the white leaves through his hand as he began to speak, his voice rising cavernous, Delphic, over the faint white flutter not yet silenced.

"I look around here and see what we call 'black' men; yet except for one or two of you, you represent—if I were to line you up, the widest possible spectrum between cream and coal. . . . Now you just think about that. I mean think about it some *more*. I know you've thought about it from time to time—when you wanted to get into a hotel or to have a drink in a private 'club,' or buy a home out on Northlawn, Southlawn, Eastlawn, or Cherrylawn . . . " (The group laughed; everybody knew that there had been a riot in the northern section of Detroit when a Negro had purchased a house on Cherrylawn two years ago) . . . "Nothing but ten thousand dollar houses costing forty thousand out that way are there? —for *black* folk like you.

" . . . Yet how black *are* you? Look all around you for a minute! Now look at *me*. I'm as red as an unripe plum . . . *Uh* huh! And you know why they're so many colors here? Anybody here not ashamed to tell why that is? Because that old white Devil, who won't let a black man sit beside him in the restaurant, *lusted* after our mothers, that's why . . . spilled in her his 'wicked seed' as our good black brother from Boston says in that truly great song of his, *A White Man's Heaven is a Black Man's Hell* . . . Well, isn't it?

"But now it's time to separate ourselves *out*, so that we can mingle and blend and melt again in a *black* melting pot— so all of you—Cream, Cocoa, Coal—COLORED, can become as black as your ancestors in that richest of all continents—

Africa, where there once flourished the greatest culture mankind has ever known. . . .

"Yeah. You maybe didn't know that did you? You maybe didn't know that while white men were still crawling around on their hands and knees we had already built empires. *Empires.* That's what we have to be proud of. *That's* what we have to be proud of. That's what our African brothers know about *us* that we've forgotten. Because the white man stole from us our heritage. Because we have been denied. Denied our birthright. Denied knowledge of our origins. Denied our language. Cut off from our roots. Packed in ships like vermin, so that over sixty million of us were murdered, crucified before they could even land a few million of us in this country. And then, when they got us here, they taught us their so-called religion, about a so-called *merciful* God. A god of LOVE! A god who taught that *By their fruits ye shall know them.* Well, we know them. We know that strange and bitter hanging fruit . . . And we have found their religion to be a religion of hate-the-black-man. For what else but Devils could have plowed the black sea at night with the bodies of over sixty million corpses. Have you ever seen Turner's picture, *Slave Ship?* Well, go and look at it sometime. Look at those helpless, manacled hands sinking for the last time into the white crest of the sea. Oblivion. Oblivion for them, and yet the survivors who were 'rescued' and sold into slavery learned to *envy* their horrible death . . . No god of love here. No mercy here. Nothing but murderers, rapists, plunderers, dealers in human flesh, bargainers in carrion —lower than cannibals: because cannibals at least killed only their enemy, but these hypocrites had murdered the fathers of the very slaves to whom they taught Christianity, murdered these innocent black folk who were no man's enemy. . . .

"We have never been anyone's enemy. We have been brainwashed into believing that the luckiest stroke from Heaven was precisely this mass, *forced* migration which made us so-called Christians instead of 'heathens.' They taught us a religion of acceptance. They taught us a religion of submission, a religion of loyalty, of gratitude to the blue-eyed Christ. And while they were hypocritically teaching us to turn the other cheek, what, oh my beautiful *sacred* black brothers and sisters, what were they doing? Were they turning the other cheek? No! They were burning us, raping us, lynching us . . .

"Let's go back a bit. Some of you may not know it, but *in this very city* about twenty-five years ago the sacred prophet of Allah passed through here, in the modest disguise of a seller of silks. Now you know what a *silk* is? Nobody has to tell you what a silk is. Everybody knows what it means; it means a *white* man. And why did he come in the disguise of a seller of silks? A mystery . . . like everything related to the Master, to Wallace D. Fard who came here to Detroit in nineteen hundred and thirty-one who himself was born into the tribe of Muhammed ibn Abdullah, the great Arabian prophet . . . He came here to save the black man, a seller-of-silks, that is to say *of the white man*—he came here to the Honorable Elijah Muhammed. He came as the One we awaited, our Savior. . . . But during the three and a half years before he vanished, never to return, he taught our Honorable Elijah Muhammed the secrets, the truths so bound up with one another in both the Bible and the Koran. . . . "

As Marcus X hammered away at the theme of Mr. Yacub and his creation of the white devil—whose reign after six thousand years was apparently about to crumble in some sort of retributive apocalypse—Yasha turned to stare unbelievingly at Liza.

Her eyes were wide, unblinking—sightless with conversion. Did *his* Liza, Liza of the fierce judgments, of the ironic incandescences burning with her own bitter truths—could Liza really believe all that stuff? The mythic creation, the wild eschatology? To imagine Liza bowing to the East five times a day was absurd, to imagine her bowing to a man in the person of the Honorable Elijah Muhammed, was unthinkable.

" . . . Those of you for whom this is your first call to the vision of the Honorable Muhammed," Marcus X continued after a pause, "the teachings of Master Fard, the fulfillment of the Word of Allah, let me ask you right now to begin *this minute* to live according to His instruction. Give up pork which makes your mind rancid with pork fat,

148

puts poisons in your blood. Promise yourselves to begin a new life. No more filthy pork. No dope, no alcohol, no tobacco. Start by giving up these poisons. When you've cleansed your body of these poisons, you'll be ready for the discipline of the Muslim way of life. Remember: the followers of Allah avoid fornication, gambling, quarrelling, lying, and stealing . . . and they *work*, work hard. Your labor shall make you *free*. Never let it be said of any of us that a Muslim is afraid of an honest day's work . . .

"Until then, let me pray with you all in the name of Allah. All honor is due to Allah, the Lord of the Worlds, the Master of the Day of Judgement. I bear witness there is no God but Thee and the Honorable Elijah Muhammed is Thy Apostle. . . . "

When he had finished, there was a faint rustle of skirts, a clearing of throats. Brother Sundiata X approached the lectern again to say a few words in parting; then he bowed and dismissed them.

As they stood by the doorway after the service, Yasha stared questioningly at Moseley who merely grinned and strummed his lips in a playful gesture, at once thoughtful and provocative. "Let's go," Moseley said. "I want to talk to *la belle dame sans merci* before she gets away."

The congregation began slowly filing out into the black summer night; it had rained while they were inside, and although the sidewalks were washed clean, the streets were filled with refuse floating along the curbs toward the swollen gutters. He and Moseley waited several feet from the door of the mosque for Liza; she was moving very slowly down one of the aisles, arm in arm with one of the black sisters. . . . When she saw him, she and the woman with her turned quickly in the opposite direction. Yasha refused to believe that she would actually turn her back on him, and began to walk rapidly toward her now hastening figure. Moseley followed them.

"Liza," he called sharply, and was gratified to see her pause and wait. He noted how she slid her arm into that of her companion, drawing closer to her, dissociating herself from the two approaching men.

"Liza, you might at least let an old friend speak to you a minute," he said reproachfully. He was not quite close enough to speak without raising his voice, and he regretted the embarrassment he must be causing her by seeming to shout at her in public. He tried to drop his voice as he added, "Liza, darling." Liza's eyes narrowed with rage as if he had insulted her. He was startled by a swift movement of her hand, a wide, swinging motion aimed directly at him. He backed away, but not before her hand had left a stinging burn on his cheek. While he stared at her in wonder, he heard an echo of satisfaction go through the curious, watching congregation.

"White devil!" Liza hissed and hurried away, her black heels clicking furiously against the rain-washed streets.

Moseley took him by the arm and led him away, but from time to time Yasha would turn around in bewilderment, seeking Liza's invisible, fleeing figure. Although the blow Liza had dealt him no longer hurt him, he held his palm to the spot almost tenderly; for he hoped it would set him free.

Only of course he should have known that where there is guilt and love there is no freedom: if character was fate, his love for Liza was as inevitable as the catastrophe in the fifth act. It was almost as if Papa had known years ago when he, Yasha, had first begun eating at "soul" restaurants and giving free "medical" advice to his black friends (while still an ignorant student he had felt qualified to suggest causes for symptoms with an audacity which today as a licensed physician he could rarely summon) that Yasha was binding himself irrevocably to Something. Symptoms as endemic as those of the common cold: eating in black restaurants, falling in love with Liza.

So he now found himself outside her apartment, pacing back and forth, rehearsing what he would say to her, what she would say to him in reply, and how happily it would all end. . . . Except that he knew even as he stood there that Liza would never reply as he had prepared her speech in his private scenario: he could rely only upon her unpredictability. She would become suddenly intellectual when he expected her

to be purring contentedly in his arms; or at the theater she
would suddenly begin to knead her fingers along his thigh
at a moment of high drama on the stage—at the scene between Hamlet and Gertrude for instance.

He sounded the buzzer, but did not pick up the speaker.
He heard her mellow voice ask, "Who is it?," then repeat more
sharply, "Who *is* it?" He figured she would either buzz the
lobby door open or come down from her second-floor apartment to see who it was. He flattened himself against the glass
door, his hands outstretched on either side, a suppliant's pose:
he had learned a thing or two from Liza about kinetic drama.

As he had hoped, she came to the landing at the head of
the stairs; first he could see her toes, looking like pieces of
English toffee, sticking out of furred blue slippers; then a robe
the color of silverfish, one which he had given her and in
which she now glided down the stairs silent and graceful as
if he were in fact watching her through subterranean glass.

She stood on the other side of the glass doorway. A faint
cloud of moisture filled the glass on his side; she glanced at
it as if to measure its breadth. He blew on it again, wrote
quickly, in reverse: I love you, but the temperatures were not
stable, and the words rippled away in a mist of air, leaving a
kind of rainbow on the glass.

Then, thoughtfully, reluctantly, she turned the knob; he
watched it as it moved slowly, like the wheel of a ship in a
dream, the soundless waves of light on the glass. For a moment
he had a vision of himself and Liza afloat on this sea of light
and glass—Liza at the helm, turning, turning into tropical
silences: two ancient mariners adrift.

She held her robe tightly around her as he entered. Without a word she let him follow her upstairs; he was somehow
grateful for that—no childish scene in the hallway, no yelling
to passersby to get this thorn of a white man out of her flesh.

He was somehow surprised at the lavishness of her sur-
roundings; no, not lavishness but a subtle sensuousness revealed
in the woven tapestry on the wall, in the African fertility
sculptures on the bookshelves. A thick carpet of black sheep-
skin lay in the center of the room before the open fireplace;

and above the fireplace, a painting of what seemed to be an army of black people. They were not dressed as soldiers, however, he noted at once; clothed only in simple white coats, above which their shining eyes and black heads moved forward as through a phalanx of darkness till the perspective reared up before the viewer's eyes, larger than life. In front were those who were clearly the leaders, resembling no leaders that he knew: it was not a hall of fame; their hands were manacled, their feet were in chains, but it was obvious they were leading all the same.

On the coffee table lay an open Swahili dictionary. . . .

At the sight of all this Pan-Africanism, not theatrically displayed, but simply permeating the atmosphere of the room, like blood in one's veins, Yasha inwardly groaned. He knew there was nothing he could offer to transcend this heritage: it must be for Liza like being the beautiful orphan in a fairy tale where one's father turns out to be King of all the Land.

Yet his deepest surprise came from Liza herself. She was looking at him silently, but not guardedly: it was a silence neither suspicious nor reproachful, but seemed, wholly, a kind of repose, a pervasive calm. He had thought he would, first of all, tell her he was sorry about the baby. Surely in her eyes that was his worst crime, and if they crossed that hurdle, they could perhaps . . . love one another again? Looking at Liza's scrubbed face, with her brown-and-gold eyes resting on him as though he were a film and she only an observer, he was not sure what he should do first. He remembered how one Friday evening during the past summer, when he had known the Muslim services were being held, he had deliberately taken an after-dinner walk past the little store front congregation on Frederick Street known as the Mosque of Islam Number One. That evening Liza had come out of the Mosque, talking in a lively, affectionate way to a Muslim sister beside her. Upon seeing him, she had turned silent, acknowledging his presence there by a widening flicker of her eyes which had seemed to him, in the mellow twilight, the color of bright yellow leaves. He had experienced the oddest surge of astonishment and desire at the sight of Liza with her champagne-tinted wig put

aside and her hair in the new style, a stunning wooly crown. In her ankle-length white dress she might have been a Moslem woman walking the streets of Damascus. . . . He had stood there staring into her eyes, noting with naive surprise that Liza's skin, washed clean of rose-tint powder was precisely the color of sun-bleached clay.

At that instant's silent exchange, Liza had turned to the Muslim sister and had begun talking in a quiet voice—only slightly breathy in the empty street. Yasha had hurried on, feeling iconoclastic, rootless: and envious. Liza had been taken from him and joined in bonds of love and hate to seven hundred and fifty million other dark-skinned people (not even counting the Chinese): in bonds of love for those who like herself were either brown or black or yellow, in bonds of hate toward those who like himself, were "white." That was what he found himself unable to grasp. Once she had loved him deeply and now he had become a part of her demonology, the White Devil in an apocryphal text.

Recalling their last meeting, Yasha now said cautiously: "I was afraid you might not let your White Devil in your house."

She smiled vaguely—not at him, but at some faraway object: at the leader in the painting perhaps. "Well, you *are* a devil: but perhaps not exclusively because you're white."

This was encouraging; in spite of her composure, he thought he saw a restless movement of legs beneath her robe, and his impulse was to throw himself dramatically at her feet, begging her to forgive him. But that was not his style; he could no more do that than he was capable of beating her lovely, stubborn head in: yet in her eyes he was a murderer.

"You have a nice place here," he said, smiling involuntarily at his own cliché.

"Little money, little time. Some help from friends."

*Bad*, he decided. What friends? Was there someone living with her? He took refuge in the thought that Muslim women were not likely to do that.

"Lots of space. Big kitchen, bath. . . . " He looked away, because he could tell by the widening of her eyes that she knew he was counting bedrooms: as if mere number could tell him what he wanted to know.

"You didn't come here for a real estate estimate," she observed sharply, in her old manner. "So quit jivin' me, Yasha, and tell me what you want."

"You."

She waited, as if his sentence had only just begun. So he repeated: "You. I want you."

She pulled her robe around her in a gesture which in the old Liza would have made him smile for its incongruity; but he knew enough to realize that Islam demanded modesty of its women. He was relieved to see that although her hand moved as if to protect her robe, her eyes dilated, glowed. He could even see her sharp intake of breath, the swelling of her breasts . . . Goddamned perpetual physician that he was, he could virtually take her pulse while his mind wandered to what she would do if he took her in his arms. But they were separated by the wide expanse of sheep-skin: if he were to get up suddenly, she would at once be put on the defensive against him.

"Listen," she protested, as if suddenly remembering to be angry: "if you've come here to see if you can climb back into bed with me, you're one hell of a white asshole—" She bit her lip in annoyance with herself: evidently such language was something she was cutting out of her new role.

"If that's what you call it, my loving you. . . . " She turned her head away as if determined not to look at him. "I came here to tell you I'm sorry . . . About the baby, I mean. . . . "

She put out her hand—not toward him, but pushing him psychologically away. "Don't . . . Don't talk about that. . . . " Tears flooded her eyes with terrific suddenness. He had to accept the fact that though many months had gone by, her loss was still too keen for him to touch upon. Yet almost at once her manner changed; by some mysterious alembic she transformed her pain into rage: "What the hell right do *you* have to talk about it?"

He sat mute. Finally he said: "I don't have any rights." Sadly he added: "That's the whole point. I don't have any rights whatsoever to declare over you. And philosophically at least, I try to persuade myself you don't have any rights over me. *Freedom now*, you know?" he dared to smile wanly, hoping she would look at him. But she only took out a handkerchief and blew her nose noisily (it occurred to him that he had never seen Liza do that: it was as if she had never allowed him to see her do any "unattractive" thing, however natural). "Only I guess you do . . . " he went on, trying consciously now to remain "humble": " . . . *do* have some rights over me. But because I don't know exactly what they are, our ethical roles toward one another have become very muddy. . . . "

"Oh shit!" exclaimed Liza. "What kind of ethics does it take to figure out, you don't go around killing off black babies. *Infanticide*, that's your ethical role."

"O.K., you said it. That's what I wanted you to come out and say: *black* babies. You're sure one hell of a fanatic if you think the reason I don't care to be a *parent* is that I don't want *black* kids. Now really: 'infanticide' is really pretty far out, even for . . . even for a Muslim."

He was surprised that she did not lash out at him for the condescension he could hear in his own words: instead she began blotting the tears as they rolled down her cheeks.

"Not just the Muslims are against it. Christians too. You seem to forget I was a church-going Baptist long before I ever even *heard* of Dr. Yasha Kalokovich. "In fact," she added with a kind of irrelevant resentment, as if it were something she still held against him—that they had lived together and there were things he did not know about her, questions he had failed to ask. "We used to go to church *every* Sunday. I was baptized soon as I got to be twelve years old . . . Total immersion. . . . We had singing like it was Christmas . . . I committed myself to a life free of sin. . . . " she added without smiling to include him in any irony there might have been in her words. It was as if now that she and Yasha had separated, she no longer cared what he thought of her—no longer cared whether she appeared to him in these present reminiscences to have been even more than he had ever realized the typical black girl from the South—brought up in Alabama-ignorance, with all the hang-ups: a white father whom she had never seen, a black mother who believed that smoking, drinking, dancing, sex-ing and other Sins, were a relentless progression to perpetual Hell. He realized she had never talked about these things—perhaps because she had believed it would have made her seem in his eyes pitiably diminished: ignorant, hidebound, a caricature of a plantation-pickaninny. . . . "Above all," she added, looking at him challengingly, as if expecting him to laugh at her, "we were taught that God is Love. . . . "

Yasha sighed with relief: at least from this point they could begin to communicate: "Well, dammit, we're in agreement. If there *is* a God, he's sure as hell a God of love and not a God of hate: such as your Honorable Elijah saith that he learned from some cat named Fard—the Great Lord Fard. . . . " He had gone too far, he saw at once; he had been too audacious.

She bristled. "You don't have to make fun of it just because you don't understand it."

"Look Liza. or Sister Elizabeth, or whatever you call yourself these days—" But mockery was indefensible, so he apologized quickly: "Excuse that, I didn't mean to do that. But listen to me a minute. You know I hate to pull rank. I hate to remind you I've been reading and trying to fill my head with something besides bullshit for at least a generation longer than you have . . . " Her scornful look did not wither him at this point; it was a fact and they both knew. He blessed the incontrovertibility of simple truth. . . . "And that religion they're peddling isn't even Muhammedism. After all, Muhammedism is a very respectable faith. Millions of people practice it. But what are *you?* You're an Afro-American, dammit. That's what you are. As American as jazz and ham and eggs for breakfast. But besides that, there's a very simple tragic flaw in it all. I happen to accept the teaching that no good fruit can come from a bad tree. And a tree that teaches that most of the human race, just because it's *white* is your enemy, that teaches that you, *personally, you* Liza, have to hate them and avoid them, and produce more and more black babies in order to compensate for the white man's 'genocide'—well: baby, whatever else you might have given up when you stopped believing in hard-core Baptist, did you give up *love?*"

158

Her chin fell slightly, and she folded her hands with an odd air of innocence which almost put him back to the notion of throwing himself at her feet and asking pardon; but he went on hopefully: (Dr. K, he admonished himself, always in favor of reasonable argument over melodrama): " . . . and love's all we've got. Not just we, I mean. Not that kind of love. Love just like on the backyard fences. L-O-V-E as in godislove, that's what's going to save us from the nuclear holocaust: and nothing else. Not Islamism, nor Pan-Africanism, nor the state of Israel, nor Communism, nor the United Nations, but just *love*. And you better believe it!"

He took a deep shuddering breath; he had not realized himself how much he believed it, till he was forced to put his future on the line, as it were, and persuade someone he loved that it was so. "And that's why white people like me are going down South to break the color line. Me and Moseley, we're leaving together for the first sit-ins. Later we've got some bus rides planned . . . Some of us may get our heads bashed in. . . . " He paused. He didn't want payment in advance for "heroic service." "And there're plenty of whites going to be in this thing. It's not that white people going South for the black man's liberation is the biggest thing since Moby Dick; but it's a *start*, and we have to start *some*place. . . . I learned that the hard way," he added humbly. "I copped out on Moseley during the Montgomery boycotts: I really didn't believe Moseley when he said *love* had the power to overcome the stench of prison. I'd had *enough* of prison. . . . But maybe it does. Maybe he's right. Anyway, I'll have to find out for myself." He smiled apologetically. "The existential man . . . y'know?"

But she had fallen into a sullen silence; he feared she had tuned herself out and had stopped listening at some point in his pleading.

Finally she said: "So you're going down there—to integrate crackers with black folks? . . . " She added, avoiding his eyes: "Just how you going? Disguised as a Confederate soldier? You know you going to get your head busted again."

"We're going to sit in the restaurants till we shut them all

down if we have to . . . Then we're going to get buses. . . .
Take 'Freedom Rides'."

She looked up angrily. "Now isn't that truly wonderful! Now
at last all those Uncle Toms will be able to sit down next to
a white man" (she folded her hands in mock reverence) "and
drink a cup of coffee. . . . "

"That's not the point. The point is we're *doing* something
together. We're joining together in lawful protest."

" 'Lawful protest,' shee-it. So some big brute of a 'deppity'
can come along and shoot all those white brains of yours right
out of your head?"

"Are you worried? Are you worried about me?" he sensed
that he should not have asked that: it would send her flying
back to the Muslim barricades.

"Why should *I* care what ideas a white man has about
other white men? Those crackers are just fascists. If you want to
go down there and pretend they're Christians, and that they're
going to come lick *love* right out of your hand like at Holy
Communion or something, that's your . . . funeral. What my
people need is not to drink coffee at a white man's counter in
Alabama, but to grow it—in their *own* state—"

He cocked his head attentively. "Is that what you . . .
they—want?"

"What they . . . *we* want is to get as far away from white
people as possible. Have our own land, our own culture, our
own banks and capital and everything . . . "

"*Another* capitalist state? You'll soon have a class of
wealthy black people living off the sweat of other black people."

"I don't understand nuthin' about that, white-boy," she retorted suddenly in her old style. "What I do know, is I'm going to Africa, and for all I know, I may *never* come back. . . . "

His heart sank. If she was going to disappear into her his-
toric past, whether real or mythic, he would never be able to
find her again; they would never be able to touch common
ground. He suddenly realized he had been stupidly negligent.
Although compared to himself, Liza was a child, she was extremely intelligent and, above all, educable; he should have
flooded her with books instead of caresses. Now, like any

child deprived of "love," she had turned upon him as a symbol of the institutions which had rejected her. He apprehended all this in one of those flashes of insight by which one's vision or honesty, after months of wilful blindness, is restored, but at the moment it was too late to do anything about it except to plead in the name of the familiar emotions—"love," "fidelity," "family." So he said as tentatively as possible, so as to make it sound as if it were merely a philosophical point he was offering: "Liza, I think we should get married. . . . " He paused before he added: "Don't you?" He was prepared for anything, for laughter, bitterness, melodrama, for an excoriating, "Get off my back, Whitey," for anything except this strange and gentle detachment. She looked at him a long time; her amber eyes seemed to move toward him like a small doe's in the darkness, but she scarcely moved. "Why?" she said.

He took a deep breath, trying not to sound like the Learned Doctor she always took offense at: "Because unfortunately, marriage is a *social value*; I feel it's merely a contract between two consenting persons. But society has made such a fuss about it, that it's taken on a mystical meaning above and beyond its true significance. Follow me?" he asked involuntarily. She hated to be asked if she understood, especially when they were talking about what involved *her* emotions, *her* life, *her* future. "In short, if the damned paper license means a license-to-love: O.K., I'm for it. I love you; *therefore* let's hurry down to the city hall and get a license . . . to love. Then we can drive over the state line and be married as soon as we can pick up a j.p. somewhere to say the words."

Liza stood up nervously; he saw that her calm had become something she was invoking; it no longer came easily. She picked up one of the African fertility dolls and sat down abruptly on the floor, in the center of the soft, dark rug. She lay the doll in her lap like a child and unconsciously rocked it. "But I'm going to Africa," she murmured. "It's impossible. I can't get married. I can't marry you . . . I have to see Africa. I have to see . . . my people."

"For God's sake, Liza. You just told me yourself your people attended the Baptist Church every Sunday, that they never

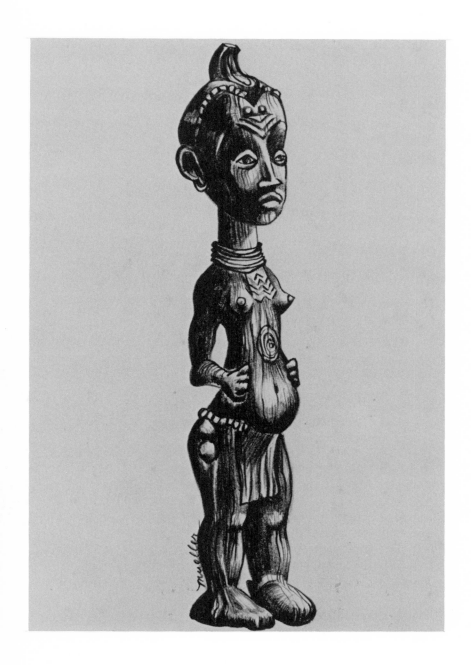

162

danced, smoked, touched liquor or committed adultery. That
they believed in Sin and at the same time that God-is-love.
Now what the hell is Africa to you?"

Without a sound she rose to her feet and took a small
green book from her shelf; she opened it to a familiar place
and read in a tremulous voice, without once looking up, as
though she were reciting a litany in which he had no part . . .
"*What Is Africa to Me? . . .*"

> What is Africa to me:*
> Copper sun or scarlet sea,
> Jungle star or jungle track,
> Strong bronzed men, or regal black
> Women from whose loins I sprang
> When the birds of Eden sang?
> *One three centuries removed*
> *From the scenes his fathers loved,*
> *Spicy grove, cinnamon tree,*
> *What is Africa to me?"* . . .

When she had finished, she shut the book softly, decisively,
but did not lay it aside. She did not ask him if he had understood it; it seemed enough for her that it was her particular
piece of music. . . .

But he felt he had understood all too well. Africa was
something vast which belonged to her and from which he
was automatically excluded; since he could never claim to have
been born there, he was by *birth* excluded from that nobility,
that hierarchy, that new caste. It was instant power, redemption,
identification with Greatness. He would not have deprived
her of her faith in Africa any more than he would have deprived Mama of her belief that all men were good, good, good:
you only had to find the key to open their goodness. As Mama
had kissed the mezzuzah every time she had crossed their lintel,
believing in everything, in signs and portents, demons and
angels, in God and mezzuzahs and above all the beauty and

---

*From Countee Cullen's *On These I Stand,* "Heritage" (New York:
Harper and Brothers, 1947).

redemption of man, so Liza believed in Africa: it was a belief in Beauty itself, and what right had he to diminish that?

Yet he tried, once more, to win at least a paper victory. "And getting married? Does getting married enter into it? After all, Richard Wright married a white woman, didn't he? And took her to Africa?"

Her eyes widened a little with surprise. "Would you go?"

"No," he admitted. "Never. What could I do in Africa? It'd be suicide for me . . . I've a job to do *here*. And we're setting out to do it, Moseley and I . . . Will you still be here? . . . In the States, I mean, when we get back?"

She rose from the carpet and carefully restored the fertility doll to its place on the shelf: "But when are you leaving?" she asked, without turning to look at him.

"Couple of months. When we can get things arranged: somebody to take over for me at the hospital, insurance policies. . . . "

"Oh," she said tonelessly, then turned toward him with a sigh which resembled resignation. "Oh, I'm not likely to be gone then. I'm just at the money stage . . . When I can get enough together, and it's got to be enough to keep me over there awhile, then I can *begin* to get with it on the other things, the visa and the passport and all those shots you have to take—"

"What you're saying," he interrupted harshly, "is that when you're ready, you'll take off—and to hell with me, right? And that, if you happen not to have gone yet when Moseley and I get back, why then I'll see you? . . . " He was not certain himself which of his questions he wanted answered.

Liza avoided both questions by saying unexpectedly, "Write to me, Yasha, will you? Let me know you're . . . safe."

"What for?" he demanded bitterly. "So you can run off to Africa and forget a living man instead of a dead one?"

But as she stood in her doorway, raising her hand toward him in mute but somehow affectionate farewell, he began to feel perhaps it had been a kind of victory that she didn't hate him enough to want to see him killed: perhaps that was all a white man could ask.